All That Glitters

by

Alisa Valdes-Rodriguez

* * * * *

PUBLISHED BY:

Alisa Valdes-Rodriguez

All That Glitters

Copyright © 2010 by Alisa Valdes-Rodriguez

* * * *

Mackenzie

I kneel on the dull wooden floor of the musty school gymnasium.

"Okay, girls," I call. "On your own this time. Ready?"

The eighteen members of the Mariposa High School dance team scurry to their places and flash those on-stage smiles at me. Half of them have braces. I run my tongue over the fronts of my now-smooth top teeth and remember the "braces" phase of my own life, and wonder what the future holds for these kids.

I press play on the bulky black CD player, and the girls explode into a synchronized blur of kicks, leaps, flips and shimmies, nailing the high-energy routine set to a popular song. They wear basic sweatpants and T-shirts, but I can see exactly how tight this machine has gotten these past few weeks, how exciting and unexpected this routine will be once they're in uniform at the statewide competition.

Watching them thrills me. I smile to myself, flooded with pride. My girls – and that is how I think of them – amaze me. Here they are, on a Saturday afternoon, in their free time, working hard to perfect their routine. Certain people (my mother, for instance) are too quick to underestimate kids from Magnolia Park. But my mother –

Mrs. Suzi-with-an-i de la Garza, former Miss Texas runner-up and current Houston socialite – is another issue for another day. Actually, she's a whole monkey-barrel of issues. I don't want to think about her right now. How is it she manages to invade every moment of my life? For now, I want to bask in the warmth of this hard-earned pride, to watch my girls dance like joy has always been theirs, like they have no worries, like victory is imminent. Like they finally believe, as I do, that they matter to the world.

I've been the dance team coach here since I graduated from Rice two years ago, and in that time this school has soared to close to the top in the state. I think we've got a heck of a good chance of taking state this year. The Houston Chronicle headlines have said things like "Where'd They Come From?" and I've answered – to myself only, of course – they came from deep in the heart of Texas. They came from good old-fashioned hard work. They came from sweat and dedication, like any other outstanding athletes. I want to feel good about how streamlined they look right now, turning and flipping with the precision of a school of fish. I want to enjoy this moment, as I imagine what the state of Texas will think when a dance team from an East Houston public school takes the state championship for the first time. All American girls. These kids can do it. I know they can.

Sadly, the happy moment doesn't last long. Halfway through the song, the stained white plaster of the ceiling cracks open like a rotten egg, and a putrid waterfall cascades down upon the team from above. The girls shriek and scatter. The water rains down, with something brown and moving in it. What is that? Cockroaches? God, no. Really? Sickening. Instinctively, I yank the cord for the CD player out of the wall and jump up to herd the girls together in a safe, dry place in the darkened hall just outside of the gym. "Over here! Quickly now!"

The girls hurry out into the hall, some on the verge of crying while others are almost laughing. I see this unusual reaction in a lot of these kids, this laughing in the face of fear and danger. I don't even like to imagine what kind of a life a kid has to have had to get to that point.

"Is everyone okay?" I ask. I count them. Eighteen. All here. No one hurt, thank God. A few of the girls are a bit wet, but that appears to be all. They're chattering among themselves, disbelieving but unsurprised, like they want to be disgusted that their school is falling apart but aren't quite sure that sort of emotion is allowed. At this school, as in many of their homes – our homes, really – quiet obedience seems to be the only valued personality trait in girls.

"Miss de la Garza?" asks my star dancer, a graceful, powerful, soft-spoken junior named Samantha. "What do you want us to do?"

Samantha's parents took out a fifteen-thousand dollar loan for her Sweet Fifteen party but have not saved any money for her college tuition, even though she has a passion for chemistry.

I look her in the eye and swallow down the words I long to say: I want you to protest in the streets for better schools. I want you to hold your representatives accountable for providing you with the same kinds of schools in East Houston as I had access to growing up in Piney Point Village. You should demand and demand and demand, until someone listens to you – and if they don't hear what you're saying after that, you should demand louder. You should demand that your parents fight the illegal redistricting of the city that took power away from them. You should scream, and fight for what you're worth in this world. Not that I do this in my own life, of course, but like The Bible says, it's always easier to see the speck of dust in another person's eye than it is to see it in your own. I am no one to judge anyone else, but sometimes it is awfully hard not to.

I smile sorrowfully at her, knowing that if I said all those things I'd lose my job. Honestly? I wouldn't feel it much, financially. This job pays very little. I still live with my parents as a result, in the comfortable four-bedroom suburban Houston home where I grew up. Mostly, I save my income for the day when I might actually move out. That's not entirely true. I also use some of my money for photography supplies for the darkroom I've built in my brother Greg's old bedroom, and that's about as far as it goes. See, I have a bigger reason to want to keep this job. If I lost this job, this team would lose the state championships. I'll quit, eventually. Or get fired. But not just yet. It's all about timing.

I smile at Samantha. "Let's just call it quits for today. You girls go get dried off, and then head on home. I'll take care of all this mess."

"You sure?" Samantha looks eager to help. At potlucks for the team, I've watched as she served her older brothers plates of food, the dutiful sister. She deserves so much more from life. So much better.

I nod, and pat her on the shoulder. "Go on home, now, sweetie."

"But our stuff," she says apologetically, her eyes turning toward the gym. Of course. Their purses and backpacks.

"Wait here." I hurry back in, and gather their things, praying the ceiling won't fall down upon my head. It takes three trips, but I get it all. They thank me, and I assure them that it's all going to be okay, even though I don't quite believe it myself.

As I watch them gather themselves to go, accepting of the subhuman conditions in which they are forced to prepare for their adult futures, many because they don't realize it can be any different, my heart breaks. There's got to be something I can do about this rotting gym, I think. I reach into my handbag and pull out my camera. I glance behind me to make sure no administrators are around. I don't need them to know that underneath my cheerful exterior is a serious journalist waiting to be born.

I remove the lens cap, focus and shoot – the water, the ceiling, the roaches, the girls as they walk with bruised pride and strong, steady shoulders toward the dented metal doors that lead back out into the hot, humid air of Magnolia Park, to their other lives. The lives my mother doesn't think are worth the effort to change, because she thinks people here choose to struggle.

The lives I wish I could rescue them from.

My cell phone rings. It's my mother, reminding me to pick my brother Greg up at the airport in an hour. He's flying in from Austin and staying with us until Monday, just to play in a father-son golf tournament with dad tomorrow at the gorgeous private club to which our family belongs. It costs thousands of dollars just to register for the event, which raises money for cancer research. I assure my dear mother that I haven't forgotten about Greg. I try to sound cheerful, but the truth is, I feel sick as I end the call. I feel sick because life just isn't fair. At all. And somewhere, for some reason, I feel like that's all my fault.

Zora

I march – as well as anyone can march in a pair of strappy black open-toe $2000 Ferragamo pumps and a black Chanel power suit ($8000, but who's counting?) that suddenly feels too hot for Houston – across the slick white tiles of the George Bush Intercontinental Airport and try to ignore the growing muscle cramp in my left shoulder. I focus on the upbeat music in my earbuds. Music does wonders to distract the mind from pain. I should know. I wouldn't have gotten through my divorce without it.

I move in time to the pop music beat, and feel my hips and breasts bubble to the groove. Power suit on the outside, girly panties with cartoon characters on them underneath. That's all you need to know about me, probably. When you have to grow up too fast, like I did, you hold on to youth culture a little too long I suppose. I know I'm probably too old for this kind of music. Women in their thirties aren't supposed to love Kanye, are we? I don't care. It's a cool song. Even so, this cramp isn't going away. The paperwork is just too damn heavy.

I should have had my assistant overnight the mountain of contracts to my condo here in Houston, but I'm paranoid enough to worry they'd get lost. When you're talking about hundreds of millions of dollars, you're better off taking the paperwork with you, in your bulging vintage crocodile

Hermes attaché case, even if said paperwork collectively weighs only slightly less than a two-year-old child; nearly thirty pounds of paper, suspended from a little strap over my left shoulder. Just call me Zora the Iron Agent. Then call the masseuse and make me an appointment.

I take one earbud out, replace it with my Bluetooth earpiece. I dial my office. Tara picks up after three rings, too many rings. I've told her, two rings maximum, but does that girl ever listen to me? No.

"I just landed," I tell her, skipping any pleasantries.

"How was your flight, Miss Jackson?"

"It went up and came down, like all of them. About the call with Billy-"

"You want me to get Billy on the conference call now, Miss Jackson?" She is interrupting and chomping, sloppy chomping of food in my ear. Tara's eating something. At her desk. Chewing with her mouth open. She annoys me just enough not to care about making her work this weekend.

I sigh and try to remain patient with her. Five assistants in two years, and still I haven't found a great one. Or even a good one. You'd think there'd be a large pool of candidates in New York City, but nope.

"No, Tara. I can't do the conference call with Billy. Delayed flights. Remember? I'm running to make tonight's game as it is. Oh, and I need you to tell Jackie I'll be calling him in about ten minutes."

"Yes, Miss Jackson."

"Gotta go."

"Wait, Miss Jackson?"

"Yeah?"

"Sports Illustrated called and said Dominick's not cooperating with them on the photo shoot stuff."

"Why the hell not?"

"He wants to hand-pick the photographer and approve the photos himself."

"Fine. I'll talk to him. Thanks."

I end the call without saying goodbye because Tara is one of those people who likes to linger and linger on the phone with you, the need kind who have a hard time saying goodbye to anyone. I don't want to give her a chance to keep talking.

In my haste, I quite by mistake bump into someone. I turn to mumble my "pardon me" and see a thin, pretty young Hispanic woman in sweatpants and a tight, sparkly tank top that shows off her youthful perkiness. I hate her instantly, because she is just the sort of female my ex-husband would have stared at in public, in front of me. Thus, the "ex" part.

"Sorry," I tell her.

She smiles politely and tells me it's okay, and I carry on, even though it looks like she might be trying to place where she's seen me. This happens more than I'd like. I'm an agent because I like being behind the scenes, but as one of the few females in the sports-agent field, I get more attention from the press than I'd like. I peek back at her, and she's still watching me, with a puzzled look on her face. She catches me looking, and waves. Ugh. I like Texas, but, seriously, the whole hyper-friendly thing here is annoying. I prefer New York, where everyone minds their own beeswax. That said, the girl is vaguely familiar-looking to me, but then again so many of these beautiful Texas girls look alike it's hard to tell. There's a uniformity to them that is a little scary, and it doesn't matter what tone their skin is. Out here it's about long hair, fresh faces and perfect bodies. People say Los Angeles is the land of beautiful women and cosmetic surgery, but that's only because they've never been to Houston, and this city makes me think I am starting to need a little Botox or something myself.

I keep moving. I am always moving. I roll my Vuitton carryon bag through the enormous rotunda occupied by the bronze sculpture of George H. W. Bush, and laugh to myself. The statue is a riot. He looks like he's prancing down a catwalk at Fashion Week, toes pointed just so, jacket thrown every so gaily over his limp shoulder. Not, I would imagine, the look he was going for. But then, artists always have the last word, don't they? Makes me wish I'd been an artist, but there's no security in that. Financial security, I mean. You been poor and get yourself out of that nightmare, you don't much want to go back. Trust me.

I blast through baggage claim, looking for my driver but not waiting for any suitcases. The bonus of having a condo here, along with my main residence on the Upper West Side of Manhattan, is that I have a closet full of clothes waiting for me, and don't have to pack much.

Soon, I spot the man in the black blazer, holding the placard with my name and company – Zora Jackson, Zojack Enterprises – across the front. I nod to let him know I'm the woman he's waiting for. He takes the bags from me and lurches off toward the exit. A driver of few words. Thank God.

I follow him to the curb outside, into the warm, breathy fog of Houston humidity, and wait as he opens the back door of an impossibly shiny black Lincoln Towncar. I slide onto the soft black leather seat of the delightfully chilly car. He closes the door, and I check my iPhone. My daughter, the wise-guy, says I'm addicted to it. I'm not so much an addict as I am a control freak with a million things going on – a million things that are putting said wise-guy through college, thank you.

Right now, I'm juggling negotiations for three baseball players, waiting for a few top college football players who have a shot in the 1st round of the NFL draft in April, dealing with some contract issues for a problematic star NBA player, and smoothing out endorsement deals for a beautiful young Polish tennis star who looks like a more voluptuous Anna Kournikova but plays like Venus Williams.

The driver starts the ignition as I speed-dial my condo. My daughter answers. The driver says something to me, but I can't pay attention to him right now because I'm trying to figure out just how many friends my child is hosting at the condo in my absence. Hello? Did she not realize her mother was flying in today?

"Ma'am?" asks the driver, motioning behind the car at something he seems to think it urgent.

I hold up my hand to let the driver know I cannot be bothered. He gets that face going like he thinks I'm a total bitch. I really do not care.

"Just drive," I tell him. "That's what we pay you for."

"But there's a girl," he says. "Behind us."

I look out the back window. The pretty girl I bumped into earlier is running toward us, waving her arms. I sigh, because people are truly the most irritating things in my life.

"Go," I command, the New Yorker in me suspecting she wants to annoy me some more. Maybe she figured out who I am and wants to get an autograph, or tell me what a great athlete she is. I'm not in the mood.

"You're sure?" asks the driver. "She seems like she wants something."

"Go." I cut off any further questions by turning sideways, away from the driver.

I learned a long time ago that there's only so much energy to go around, and if you waste your time trying to be nice and pleasant with everyone you come into contact with – in my line of work we're talking hundreds of new people a week sometimes – you only end up drained. You need good solid walls up around you, no matter how rejected they might make others feel. The truth is I will probably never see this driver again, so I really don't have the time or energy to spend discussing his children, the weather, whatever. When I was younger I worried about making a good impression on everyone. I worried about being nice. Now, I save the good impressions and manners for those who matter. And those who matter can be counted on two hands. Maybe one. The older I get the more I understand that nice girls truly do finish last. I've seen last place. It ain't pretty.

"Sounds like a good time over there," I say into the phone.

"Mom? You here already?" I hear her cover the phone with her hand and tell her friends to "Shut up, you guys! My mom's on the phone." The din diminishes slightly.

"Just landed. Wanted to warn you I'm on the way, in case you have any bodies you want to hide."

Silence.

"See you in a few."

"Okay mom."

After we say our goodbyes and hang up, I dial Marcos, a soccer player of mine in Spain – World Cup is coming this summer, and you wouldn't believe how much these guys get paid – and share an idea for a sports drink endorsement that popped into my head during the flight. After that, I make another call. And then another. Recently, a big national news magazine named me one of the twenty-five most influential sports agents in the nation. I was the only woman on the list, and one of only ten agents who own their own firms. You don't get that kind of accolade sitting back and waiting for things to happen. You make them happen, every waking minute.

Six calls later, the driver pulls up outside my Memorial Park townhouse, directly across from a quiet, pastoral section of the park, just in time for me to see a few of my daughter's friends – an assortment of girls in sweatpants with stupid words printed across on the asses and guys with too many gold chains waggling on their scrawny necks –

jumping into their various designer cars to drive away. Rich kids. Even though Lissette qualifies as a rich kid herself, I was raised poor and have an instinctive mistrust of young people from wealthy homes – including, sadly, my own child. I take my bags from the driver, thank him, tip him, smooth the edges of my suit, and turn to go inside.

The townhouse is modern, three stories, with pale wood floors and floor-to-ceiling windows that look out to the park. I had a wonderful decorator do the interior in a modern, minimalist style, with bright colors and geometric shapes. Clean, uncluttered, just the way I like it. Museum-like, in a modern museum kind of way. Blank, so I can think. I grew up in a cluttered apartment in the South Bronx, a cluttered borough. New York is a cluttered city. I like space. I take a deep breath as I step inside, and let my attaché case drop with a plunk. I'm home.

Sort of.

Lissette smiles from her seat at the dining table. The floor plan is open and flowing, loft-like. Seated next to her are two young men. My back stiffens at the sight of them. When you've had a baby of your own at fifteen – my age when Lissette was born – when you know firsthand how impossible life becomes for teen girls once they've had children, you don't exactly love the thought of any males around your own daughter. You view this possibility the same way you might view the possibility of maggots in your breakfast cereal. Ain't gonna happen. Not on my watch. In fact, you hope your daughter will remain celibate until she retires – or at least until you do. I'm not particularly religious, but I wouldn't be heartbroken if Lissette decided to join a convent.

"Hi, mom!" Lissette smiles like a movie star. She is pretty as a panther, five-ten, ballerina-thin, with skin the shade of a raw almond. She has the same large, wide-set eyes and chiseled cheekbones as her father.

I decided it would be better for Lissette to live here in the condo during college – because for some inexplicable reason she decided to go to Rice instead of a school on the East Coast. She's been away from home, more or less on her own (if you count living alone but spending your parents' money being on your own) for more than a year now. I still can't quite think of her as an adult, but out of respect for her, I try. And trying involves a bit of a mantra: She's not a baby anymore; let it go, mama. I say this to myself a hundred times a day at least.

Both of the young men in my condo are attractive. The mother panther in me wants to therefore slash them to shreds with my razor-sharp claws. I'd enjoy the rubbery feel of their flesh under my nails. They sit with her at the dining table, gigantic feet too far apart in the way of confident, cocky young men. A few textbooks and spiral notebooks lie on the tabletop and two small slick silver notebook computers stand open and at attention. Studying. Yeah, right.

I go over to Lissette, wrap my arms around her and plant a kiss on her cheek. I still love the warm animal smell of this child's hair. I could sniff her out of a lineup blindfolded. Mine. My baby. Only not. She's not a baby anymore; let it go, mama.

"How are you, pumpkin?" I ask.

"Fine," she says, delivering a "mwa" to the air next to my face. Too cool for a real kiss for her mama. Embarrassed I called her pumpkin, too, from the expression on her face. Fine.

"Mom, I want you to meet my friends, Lorenzo Deleon and Yardbird Williams."

"Yardbird?" I ask, ignoring the other one. "That a real name?"

The boy smiles sheepishly, flashing the prettiest white teeth I've seen in a while, and says, "Yeah, it's real. My dad had a thing for Charlie Parker."

"Yardbird's an amazing sax player, mom," says Lissette. She's not fawning, is she? She best not be fawning. We don't allow fawning over boys, do we? But then again, we don't have any control anymore. She's not a baby anymore, mama. Let it go, let it go. Sigh.

"Damn, that's your mom?" whispers Lorenzo as he looks up from the book with one arched brow. The boy looks like the kind who's so vain he plucks his eyebrows. He stares at me, slides his eyes up and down my body. If I had claws, they'd be out and glistening right about now. "You two look more like sisters."

We get this a lot, by the way. The whole "you look like sisters" jive. I used to hate it. Now I almost like it – but I prefer the men who say it to be my age, not hers.

I turn to Lissette and raise one eyebrow, with a sigh.

"I'm really tired. I'd like to rest, take a jog, eat something, decompress – in peace – before the game tonight." I glance at my Movado, give her a look. The look. A mom look. "That gives me two hours. If you and your buddies here don't mind."

She understands exactly what I'm saying. Get them the hell out of my house. Lissette rolls her eyes as she has done to me ever since I first told her "no," but complies nonetheless. "They were just leaving. Right, guys?"

The boys get up. Yardbird smiles at me and I hate myself for noticing how edible he is, for fantasizing for a nanosecond that I'll take him upstairs and seduce him. I haven't had sex in more than six months, and I'm feeling the need. But I am not, and have never been, one of those moms who sleeps with her kid's friends. Sometimes, with the caliber of male friends Lissette attracts, it's hard not to think about it. Not that I'd ever tell her. That will never happen.

"Is it true you're a sports agent?" Yardbird asks, amazed and licking his lips. He should be leaving, but instead he's walking away from the front door, toward me. Grinning.

I affect my most matronly voice. "Yes, Yardbird. It's true."

"Well," he puffs out his chest. His very muscular, tempting young chest, wrapped in a trendy, tight T-shirt that draws attention to the biceps. The big, manly biceps. The boy is hotter than hot. "You know, I'm known to play a little football myself."

He gets that distant, important look most men get when they start to tell you about themselves. Men, as a group, tend to believe they are the most fascinating things on the planet. I tend to disagree.

He says, "I mean, with me it was always do I play ball, or sax?" The faraway look is replaced by a direct eye-connect with me. Followed by a lip-lick. "Maybe you could help me decide."

"Goodbye, Yardbird," I say with a disinterested wave. People always ask me how to become great athletes, and my answer is always the same: If you have to ask me how, then you'll never be a great athlete. Great athletes are born with the talent and the drive to do what needs to be done without asking for secrets that don't exist. By the time they're eleven, great athletes already know it and spend their free time practicing against backboards, in city playgrounds, in their own backyards. Hard work is the key to success in any profession, plain and simple.

Lissette directs the guys toward the front door, silences them with her stare. She has a killer stare, this child – I mean woman – inherited from me. The young men tumble-stumble along on their sneakered, boyish feet, mumble their goodbyes, and they are gone. Next to hands, feet are the part of a man I like best. The visible parts that are so obviously different from our own. Large hands, and strong feet? Gets me every time. Lissette's dad had some killer feet. I even loved the corns.

I slip out of my torture-chamber shoes, plunk my body onto the sofa, and close my eyes. The cool air from the AC feels just right. Lissette pads over in her bare feet, sits on a chair across from me. "Sorry about that, mom. Yardbird was out of line. I'll talk to him."

"Pssh," I say with a wave of my hand. "Forget it."

It wouldn't be the first time a gorgeous young man tried to convince me he was the best athlete in America. That distinction belongs to Lissette's father, who gave me the "I'm a great athlete" talk back in middle school, with the main difference being that in Lissette's father's case, it turned out to be true.

You know, I often say I hate people who can't say goodbye properly, people who are too chickenshit to end a call. But it's hypocritical, in a way. See, there's this thing no one knows about me. Since divorcing Ivan, I haven't loved any other man. There just hasn't been room in my heart, because he's still there. True love is like that, I guess. Even when it pushes you away, and you pretend to leave, pretend to move on, the truth is you stay there, attached as a suckerfish, unable to say goodbye.

A goddamned fool.

MacKenzie

I drive my brother Greg from the airport to our house in Piney Point Village, and drop him off at the curb with an apology because I have to get back to the school to make sure everything is taken care of, flood-wise. Greg, who seems sleepy and has spoken maybe six words since I picked him up at the airport, grunts and grabs his duffle bag. He is sluggish, which seems to be his usual state since entering college, and he barely gives me a nod through his half-closed eyes before dragging his feet across the front yard where we used to play as kids, toward the door. Our mother, tidy in her white Capri pants and lavender button-down, is standing at the threshold with her hands clasped over her heart at the sight of him, her little football star. Her boy. The pride of the family, even if he is half comatose. It just doesn't get better than a son, as far as my family is concerned. Sons make the world go around. Greg pimp-walks, like his knees might not work quite right, another strange new habit he's picked up in Austin. He thinks he's all gangsta. How silly. Clearly, my brother thinks he's very cool. And clearly, our mother agrees. I'll keep my thoughts on the matter to myself.

I sigh, and pull away from the house to drive back to the school and try to get the image of my perfect mother out of my mind. Was I imagining it, or did she look disappointed in me for some reason? She often looks like that. Like I'm just not living up to whatever it is she wants me to be. It is much like the look that businesswoman from the airport gave me after a couple of papers fell out of her attaché case as she got into her car and I tried to get them back to her. She seemed like she hated me, even though I was trying to be nice. It was very strange. The papers look important, too – some kind of legal documents full of big words. Oh well.

By the time I arrive at the high school, the gym is locked up and things appear to be past the crisis stage. I park my Liberty and walk toward a group of men at the door to the gymnasium, just to be sure.

"Miss de la Garza, I think we got it under control," says the head janitor on weekend duty, a pointy-headed dark man who reminds me of a human cigar. "Go on home now."

I thank him with a smile – smiles don't cost money, and always make the day better – and walk back to my car, trying not to notice that he whistles about me to his weird colleague, the overnight security guard. I'm used to the whistling, but I'm not exactly used to it on the job. Not on this job, anyway. I don't have the energy to set them straight. The schoolyard is littered with cigarette butts and other assorted trash. So sad.

When I return to my car, I notice a small piece of pink paper beneath my windshield wiper. It must have been there awhile, but in my haste to pick Greg up, I didn't notice it.

It's a note from my Aunt Rosie, reminding me to come to her little neighborhood store later to pick up some soup she's made for one of my teammates who is out with a broken ankle. "Don't forget to bring your portfolio," it reads. "You promised!!!"

Portfolio? She makes it sound so darn official. I take photos as a hobby, and since I was a little girl I've fantasized about maybe doing it for a living, but you have to be super smart and talented for that, and you have to have a degree in photography or art or something. My degree is in exercise science. In my wildest dreams, I'd travel the world as a photojournalist with just a backpack and some comfortable shoes, documenting the injustices that don't get addressed unless someone is there to prove they happened. Rosie is the only person I've ever really told about this, and she thinks it's totally feasible. I'm not so sure. Rosie is the biggest supporter in the world of my photography habit, and sometimes I think she goes overboard to make me feel like I have real talent or something. With no kids of her own, Aunt Rosie, my mother's fraternal twin sister, has doted on me all my life – much to my mother's chagrin. Mom would rather not let people know she was related to Rosie, partly because Rosie still lives in Magnolia Park, where they grew up and where Rosie and my grandparents still live, and partly because Rosie has never dated a man in her life, and has a special lady friend who never gets invited to holiday gatherings even though they've been together for twenty years. Mom likes to pretend for her society friends that she is unfamiliar with the entire "East Houston milieu," as she puts it; she also likes to pretend homosexuals are all evil and hell-bound, even her own sister. Like I said, I try not to judge people because I myself am far from perfect, and Rosie is a kind, generous person who treats everyone with respect and who loves me. I love her back, because to me that's what Jesus would do. My mom's Jesus, I suspect, would feed Rosie to the lions.

I climb into my red Jeep Liberty and try not to notice as the hot black vinyl of the seat burns my butt. You spend your whole life in Houston, you better be prepared to handle heat. This is the number one complaint of the three major complaints people have about my hometown – heat, humidity, and traffic jams. I love just about everything else about it, though. I blast the air conditioner, and dial Rosie's store number on my cell phone as I pull out of the parking lot. No answer. She's probably dealing with a delivery. She has a degree in world history from UT in Austin, but you'd never know it from her choice of career. She runs a

Magnolia Park grocery store that bears her name, completely alone, which I think is insane. She works from six in the morning until ten at night, a habit my father blames for Rosie's lifelong lack of a husband; my dad is a smart man in many ways, but he has never been able to admit to himself or anyone else that Rosie is gay. Same with my mom; my mother says Rosie never got a husband because she's fat, which never made sense to me because there are plenty of fat women with husbands. Rosie is pretty clear about her reasons for never having had a husband, but no one in our family believes her – not publicly anyway. It's like they all think her "condition" will rub off on them if they speak it out loud, or hug her. I'll try calling her again in a little bit.

I consider going straight to Reliant Stadium, to my second job as a professional NFL cheerleader with the Ranchers, but tonight's football game won't start for a few hours and I wouldn't know what to do with myself. I already worked out this morning – actually, I taught a super-early Step aerobics class at the gym, my third job – and practiced the routine in the studio afterwards with my best friend, fellow Ranchers cheerleader Ashley Colbert. Ashley, a mechanical engineer by day, is this beautiful, tall blonde girl from Hunter's Creek Village. We have a lot in common. She and I were on the dance team together at Rice, and we were the only girls from the team to make the cut for the Ranchers. We worked hard for it, too, helping each other with the strict diet and physical training. I've never had a closer friend.

I'm totally starving and I know that if I don't eat a little something soon I might get so hungry I end up eating too much. With the pageant coming up – and the Ranchers cheerleader tryouts just around the corner (you have to try out every year even if you're already on the team) I am down to about 1300 calories a day.

I decide instead to surprise my mom and dad (and my sleepy brother) by showing up for lunch at home. Mom is totally and completely on board with the training for me. She helps me so much, and hides all the food that might tempt me so I can't find it. In her spare time, mom, who has helped me win a few beauty pageants in my time, lends herself out to other hopefuls as a beauty pageant coach. She's amazing at it too. No one is more aware of the two pounds I still need to lose in order to be an my optimum for swimsuit more than my mother.

With my stomach growling a little, I steer across town, back to the peaceful, tree-lined, curving street where I was raised. It hits me again how unfair it is that I got all this and kids like Samantha get so little. Sometimes I talk to Ashley about it, and she's completely in agreement. She's been teaching herself Spanish and she has a boyfriend from

Mexico, which totally scandalized her family at first but they're over it now.

Thank God Ashley gets it, because I would go crazy if the only person I had to talk about this with were my Aunt Rosie. My dad is cool about it, and seems to understand, but he's not one for talking a lot. He's more of a listener, which is a blessing because my mother talks enough for both of them. I hate listening to her talk about poor people, though. She grew up poor, so you think she'd have a little more sympathy, but she totally doesn't. My mom thinks only the deserving get to be rich and comfortable. She thinks her parents, who came to the U.S. from Mexico when they were teenagers and worked really hard to make a life for themselves here, are too easily distracted by the gossip in the neighborhood and all the other "lowlife nonsense" in Magnolia Park that they never got ahead. I disagree. I know rich people, and I know poor people. It's nothing but luck that determines where you fall.

Shadow and light dance on the lawns, and on the black of the street. So beautiful. There's something almost pathological about how peaceful and pretty this neighborhood is. As a child it never occurred to me that we had it better than most people. My dad comes from a family with money in San Antonio that likes to talk about how they never crossed the border because the border crossed them. Me, I liked my mom's family's house. I mean, I knew my mom's parents had a humble house, but to me it was a fun place to go because there was always something going on there. Someone was always having a party, or there was always a barbecue. I loved going there. My mother hardly took me, though, because she was ashamed of where she came from. She had what she called her "chosen family" of Village moms and pageant moms and church moms (raised Catholic, my mother decided to become a Baptist because it was more convenient in her social circle and my dad went along with it because that's what he does most of the time) and basically we just hung out with them – even at Easter and Thanksgiving. We hung out with dad's colleagues from the hospital, too, and some of my happiest memories are of playing with dolls on the floor of the living room while all the grownup men talked about medicine and my mother waltzed around making sure the hired help got dessert wines to everyone. I felt safe. And normal. Everyone was as well off as we were. I just figured everyone except my adorable grandparents lived like we did, in a large red brick home with a large green lawn and a dozen cases of soda from Costco in the garage at any given time.

As I drive toward the house I notice a big black Ford pickup truck in the driveway. I know instantly who it belongs to, because I sat in it last Sunday, like I do most Sundays. The truck belongs to Dino Solis, my boyfriend.

He's a local boy whose dad is a bank executive. Because Greg is the same age as Dino – two years younger than me – I knew about him because they used to play football together in high school. I always thought Dino was this super hot guy who'd never have any interest in me. I just sort of admired him from afar, until he noticed me a year ago or so and we started dating.

I keep driving, because I don't understand why he'd be here. Is he visiting Greg? He would have told me he was stopping by. It's very strange. I park down the street, a few houses down, and try to decide what to do next.

Dino is the starting quarterback for the Longhorns. He drives his truck three hours from Austin to Houston every Sunday to take me to dinner and a movie, depending on his football schedule. He makes the drive religiously, and has been doing so ever since we first started dating. For a moment, because it's so out of context, I think maybe the truck belongs to someone else, but then I see the Calvin decal peeing on the Oklahoma decal, and I know it can be no one else.

I walk to the front door. My dad – a literal brain surgeon, please don't tell jokes about it, he specializes in cancer he's the first to remind people that brain cancer isn't funny at all – won't be back from MD Anderson for another hour or two.

I don't bother to put the key in the door because we don't keep it locked during the day. Around here, you don't have to. I tiptoe into the living room as quietly as I can. I look at the white Victorian sofas, the plush red Persian carpets. No one here. I continue across the room, through the formal dining room with its red striped wallpaper, and on into the large French country gourmet kitchen with the view of the great room with the soaring ceiling. I can't believe what I see.

My mother, brother and Dino sit on the overstuffed casual beige sofa that faces the plasma television on the wall, their backs to me. My mother's three toy poodles sleep on the big dog bed by the fireplace, so overfed and overdressed they are too exhausted to notice me, too. The only thing facing me is dad's framed life-sized photo of Bill Bickelworth, the head coach and general manager of the Ranchers and the man my father most admires in the world, after Ronald Reagan. Around Houston, Bill Bickelworth is pretty much a legend.

Mom still wears the oxford-style button-down Martha Stewart-style shirt, purple, and her hair is up in a neat black twist. Her shirts never have wrinkles. Dino's muscles strain beneath his snug burnt orange UT T-shirt. He's holding what looks like a ring box from Tiffany, and my mother is dabbing the corners of her eyes with a tissue. My brother leans back with his mouth hanging open, and looks like he's fallen asleep with his eyes open. For a brief moment I have the strange thought that my boyfriend is asking my mother to marry him.

"So, with your blessing, I'd like to ask her." Dino's deep voice, dripping with his adorable Texas accent, is choked with emotion. My mother drops her head and buries it momentarily in her hands. Most women do this when they are despairing. My mother does it when she's overwhelmed with happiness. Very dramatic. She lifts her head and uses her hands to cup Dino's own square, masculine, clean-shaved face, her collection of costly rings flashing in the sunlight.

"Of course we'd love to have you as part of our family," my mother tells him. "I can't imagine a better son-in-law." I see her scalp move, meaning she's smiling; this is what too many facelifts do to a woman's ability to express feelings without words. "Oh, Dino."

Greg mumbles something now, I can't tell what, and slaps Dino on the back.

"Thanks, bro," says Dino.

"True dat," says Greg.

"Word," says Dino.

I feel sick, and afraid. I'd gasp, but that would require breathing.

"Do you think she'll like the design?" he asks. "I went with the one you suggested." I can see him blushing from here. "The chick at the store said this was the most popular setting. Mackenzie likes things all weird sometimes, you know, so I wasn't sure."

My mother picked my engagement ring? That doesn't seem right. I gulp, and feel ice in my veins. I crane my neck to see the ring, but can't. My mother looks at it and places a hand on her collarbone.

"It's perfect!" she says. "So elegant! Her father will be so pleased. He had a surgery this afternoon but should be here in an hour or two. It's very sweet of you to ask us for permission, Dino. Very old-fashioned."

"Yeah," says Dino, stifling a belch with his fist. "Anyway, I think I'll hit the gym and come back later. I can't ask Mackenzie to marry me without her dad's permission."

Mom looks at him and shakes her head, something she does when she's in agreement with people, as if she's amazed anyone would be smart enough to think like she does.

"Where on earth did you come from?" she asks, complimentary. "I didn't think they made men like you anymore."

"Thank you, ma'am," says Dino.

Mom's scalp twitches again, and she hugs him. As he readies himself to leave, my heart begins to race, like I'm being chased, like I've had seven hundred cups of coffee, like I'm a rabbit with a coyote on my tail.

I know, I should be ecstatic. Dino is rumored to be the first pick in the NFL Draft, after having won the Fiesta Bowl for UT last season and with a strong season performance so far. I won't bore you with the statistics, though I know them by heart. The sports radio guys in town are saying he could get a contract worth $80 million, with $45 million guaranteed, and there's a good chance he'll be drafted by the Ranchers. He's going to be rich – or should I say richer? His family already has a million-dollar waterfront estate out in Waxahachie – and, most of all, he is going to be football royalty, in Houston. He's terribly handsome, and usually a fairly nice guy. So what's the problem, you ask?

One, I'm not sure I want to ever get married. I've watched my parents fight and torment each other for all twenty-three years of my life (can you say "silent treatment" for six straight months?) and I don't want to make that same mistake. I just don't see the value in tying yourself to a man if you're not going to be totally blissfully happy and content forever and ever.

Two, I had an abortion my freshman year in college that I never told anyone except Ashley about. She went with me and held my hand while they did the horrible thing and then she held the hot water bottle on my belly afterwards and we pretended that I was doing a sleepover at her apartment because we were studying super hard for a test.

I always told myself that if I did get married it would have to be to a guy who didn't have a problem with the abortion, or at least who could accept me even though I had one. I have terrible mixed feelings about it, and sometimes I regret it. It is something I think about most days of my life, and not a decision I took lightly. I don't intend to keep it a secret from my life partner. That would be too hard. I'm still tormented by it, and my feelings on the whole issue are what you might call mixed.

Three, I think I'm still too young to get married, even though I understand what a totally amazing and wonderful catch Dino is.

Finally, there is four: I don't know if I even love Dino. I mean, I like him. We have fun together. I guess. But I don't know if he's The One. I don't even know if I'm a The One kind of girl.

My feet start to move backwards, like I've been pushed by a ghost. I turn and retrace my steps as fast as I can without making noise, and sneak back out the door. I hurry down the block, to the Liberty, hop inside, turn the key, and peel out of the driveway like there's no tomorrow.

Zora

Memorial Park, at 1466 acres the largest urban park in Texas, is supposed to be the Central Park of Houston. But having lived all my life in New York, and having spent many hundreds of hours in Central Park, I can tell you from experience that there are several key differences that go far beyond the simple fact that you can't get to Memorial Park by subway.

One: Memorial Park is pretty much hot, muggy and green all year round. Two: Memorial Park is notably devoid of homeless drunks, garbage, rats and one-legged pigeons. Three: Memorial Park has an 18-hole golf course and public croquet fields. Four: Memorial Park has off-roads dirt trails for mountain-bike enthusiasts, where cyclists maneuver moguls up to 40 feet high – in Central Park, cyclists maneuver mostly to avoid crashing into each other on the pavement. Five: Memorial Park is full of pine trees and oaks. Six: Memorial Park has a bayou. Seven: Memorial Park does not smell of urine at half-block intervals.

As I jog on top of the soft earth of one of Memorial Park's many wooded running trails, listening to my latest smooth jazz download on the iPod, I marvel at the verdant beauty of this place. People back east have it all wrong about Houston. Most of my friends and family have these ideas that Houston is a filthy city full of oil wells and cement, or that all the men wear cowboy hats and talk like hillbillies.

But the truth is, Houston is one of the greenest, most beautiful cities in the United States, with the nation's second-largest public art collection and some of the finest museums and cultural institutions on earth. You would be hard-pressed to find cowboy hats here, as it's one of the trendiest and most fashionable cities in the world. As for that famous Texan accent people like to make fun of everywhere else? Out of date stereotype. Houston is now a majority Hispanic city, just like Miami, with one in four people in this city having been born in another country – almost all of them from Latin America. You're more likely to hear people speaking Spanish in Houston than you are to hear that cultivated Texas twang.

All of this, and a tremendous variety of professional sports teams with no shortage of enthusiastic and loyal fans, is why I chose Houston as my second home. If I didn't have to be in New York for my business (which employs 12 people) I'd move here in a heartbeat. When I left New York this morning, a sooty snow had just begun to flurry across Manhattan, prelude to a slushy storm that was predicted to dump at least a foot of filthy freezing rain by tomorrow night. Glad to be out of there - even if it looks like I left a very important part of one of my contracts back at the office in New York. Tara can't find it, which is just one more reason I am going to need to fire her when I get back. She is disorganized. I need that document, but I try not to stress myself about it. Stress will kill you.

I don't have a lot of time to jog, but I force myself to cram in what I can. I like to put in at least an hour of cardio a day. I've got obesity in my family, and this tendency to pack the pounds onto my hips and lower belly. I'm in good shape, at five-six I weigh about 140 pounds, which my doctor says is just right. Beyond the health benefits of running, I savor this intensely personal time with my own thoughts, the hypnosis of repetitive motion and music – and the meditative outcome of it. I also like listening to pop music without having my daughter make fun of me. Our society thinks new music is the exclusive domain of the young, but I disagree. Music, movement, thinking. I need it. Without my daily exercise I wouldn't be half as productive as I am. When you're under the pressure I'm under, you absolutely must take time for yourself. If not, you end up depressed and overwhelmed, like I was ten years ago, when my divorce from Lissette's father was finalized and I wondered nonstop about how I'd survive emotionally without him. Sometimes, I wake up and still feel for him in the bed, shocked with the awareness that it's over. In my heart, it has never felt over. But I don't tell anyone anymore. My friends and family – and especially my mom – got really tired of me mourning a man they didn't think was worth my time.

I check my watch. Time to turn around. I think I'll pick up the pace for the rest of the way back. Been trying to incorporate some sprints at the ends of the runs. I toggle through my music, to the indie rock section, and crank it up. There is no better jogging music in the world than speed punk. I crank it up. I charge forward, my feet landing on the dirt in time to the music, and look ahead on the trail. There are hundreds, maybe thousands, of people out this evening. Houston is supposed to be the fattest city in America, but you wouldn't know it to look at the bodies zipping along this track.

Many of the people running past me in the opposite direction smile and say hello, particularly the men, which really makes me uncomfortable. I have gotten into the strict habit of not having time to look for love. It is much easier to be pitifully obsessed with my ex-husband. Men here are very forward and inviting to women. This is the one thing I don't think I would ever get used to if I moved here permanently. As a native New Yorker, I like my privacy in public. I'm not a smiler or a greeter. I'm all about boundaries and walls. Buttresses, really. For this reason, I avoid looking at the people as they approach, just in case they want to say hi. I don't say hi. I want to run.

So you might imagine my surprise when one of the strange men approaching me – I sense he's a man from the way he moves in my peripheral vision – doesn't seem to want to accept my privacy. He darts in front of me, as if to block my path, and when I, still avoiding eye contact, try to get past him, he blocks me again. He wears jeans, which is creepy for a jogging trail, and trendy new sneakers. I avert my eyes, and try to dodge him on the other side, but he's too quick. I don't look at him.

Suddenly, his hand is on my upper arm, squeezing. I'm ready to bust out my self-defense moves on him when his face finally slips into my line of vision. It's no stranger. It's Ivan Barbosa. Lissette's father. My ex-husband. The man I can't stop loving no matter how good I know it would be for me to do so. How the hell did he end up here?

"Hey, sexy," he says in his rumbly, grumbly voice, laughing because he knows me well enough to understand exactly what I thought was going on.

"What are you doing here?" I blast past him and continue jogging. Ivan lives in Los Angeles, where he plays for the Dodgers. Pacific Palisades, to be precise. I wish he'd go back there. I'll be damned if I let Ivan get in the way of my cardio. He's gotten in the way of enough of the rest of my life as it is. Bastard.

"Pumpkinface told me you were out running, and I know you well enough to know you'd be here." He jogs along side me and I can feel his smug smile. He knows me. He knows I like to do things the same way, over and over. I'm predictable. It was one of the reasons he listed for cheating on me: My predictability. I remember it well. "I like a little spontaneity in my life," he told me then. "That just doesn't happen with you."

Sadly, it's true. I function best on a schedule, with detailed lists. He knows me better than almost anyone in the world, which I suppose was why it was all that much easier for him to figure out creative ways to lie to and cheat on me throughout our ten-year marriage. He knew when I'd be home, when I wouldn't. What sorts of lies would work on me like magic. I hate him. I love him. I hate him.

I love him.

I sneak a look at him. He's let the hair at his temples go gray and it looks very good on him. Why is it that men look good with gray hair? He catches me looking at him and I turn my gaze away quickly.

"I meant what are you doing in Houston," I say, picking up the pace in hopes of losing him. "Thought you were dealing with your mom's dream house in Puerto Plata."

He matches my pace easily. Of course he does. He's as fit now as he was as a rookie at eighteen, back when he used to go for two or three hours in bed. I'd be sore for days. Happy, sure. But sore.

He says, "I was, but when Pumpkinface told me you were coming out here to do some business, and I realized I had some free time, I had this overwhelming urge to see you."

I hate when he uses my nickname for Lissette. "Pumpkinface." It's mine. That's what I call our baby. Not what he calls her. He rarely calls her at all.

I pick up the pace even more, and true to form, Ivan easily matches it, jeans and all. "Slow down," he jokes. "You don't want to hurt yourself, old lady."

"If that were true, I wouldn't have married you."

"Ouch."

My heartbeat races, less from the jog than from the fact that in spite of all my best efforts, I am still completely crazy in love with this damn fool. He was my first boyfriend, a classmate in the sixth grade, my first kiss, my first everything. He was black like me, but an immigrant from the Dominican Republic, and by far the cutest boy in the South Bronx neighborhood where we grew up. But he was so much more than that. He was smart, an honor's student, funny, and a great athlete – not surprisingly, given that he is now known as one of the best pitchers in the major leagues and, to my great dismay, has an equally outstanding rear end.

I fell for him the moment I met him in math class. He said he loved me, and I foolishly believed it. Believed it so much that when he, all of fourteen years old, asked me to prove my love for him by bearing him a child, I stupidly agreed. That's right. My teenaged motherhood was not a mistake. How pathetic is that? I thought I was grown. I was wrong. Not that I regret having had Lissette. But I regret having had her so young. Later, I learned that his request was not uncommon in the homegrown culture of the Dominican Republic's lower classes, from which his incredible talent and intellect sprang. It was almost a required part of the courtship ritual for men, meant more to prove their machismo and ownership over the woman than as any declaration of desiring to actually raise a child. A flesh-and-blood child. He never got that part. No matter what he tells people, the fact is I raised that girl by myself, with help from my mother and grandmother and God knows how many aunts and cousins and friends.

"What do you want, Ivan?" I ask.

"Don't you know what tomorrow is?" I glance at him, and he's mock-pouting, teasing. His lips shine, freshly licked. I do, in fact, know what tomorrow is. It is the day that would have been our twenty-year wedding anniversary.

I shrug. "No. I have no idea what tomorrow is."

Ivan laughs. He knows when I'm lying, just as he knows my heart belongs to him, and always has. Which is why I could never have cheated on him the way he cheated on me, even if I'd wanted to. He, however, did not view cheating as an affront to love and loyalty, but rather the God-given right of any red-blooded man. His wandering eye – and sperm – have recently caused him to lose yet another wife. His fourth. This one, a well-known beach volleyball player, left him after she discovered he'd been cheating on her with the nanny. He has two children with her, and one with each of the other wives. Soon, he'll have a child with the nanny. Six children in all, ranging in age from nineteen to fetus. Why was the volleyballer surprised? That's all I want to know. The other three wives had all left him after finding out the same kind of thing. In my case, it was one of my best friends I found him in bed with when I came home from work with the flu one afternoon. What made this number four think she was so special?

"You know I've always loved you," he says with a faint pant. I am pleased to realize the jog is winding him more than it tires me.

"Go back to Puerto Plata," I say. "Go back to your mom."

"What's your problem?" he asks me, as if he really truly cannot understand why I might find this situation untenable. "I just wanted to spend some time with the woman I love."

"Were all the others busy?" I ask. I hate myself for doing it, because I know the last thing in the world I need to do right now is engage him in any kind of dialogue -

about any of this. My therapist has drilled it into my head that Ivan likes nothing more than getting a reaction out of me, whether good or bad, because in Ivan's warped little mind it proves to him that I still love him. I could hug him, or spit on him, and it would serve the same purpose in his pathetic world. As his first love, apparently, I still have considerable influence over Ivan's self-esteem, and as long as he incites a reaction in me, he believes I'm still in love with him.

"You know I never loved them the way I loved you," he tells me. "I only married them because you dumped me."

Keep quiet, Zora, I tell myself. But I don't listen. "Because I dumped you? You make it sound like I had a choice, Ivan. But it was your fault. You know that. I didn't want my marriage to end. You gave me no choice. Your. Fault."

We've been through this same song and dance so many times I don't know why I bother. I can predict what comes next. He'll ask me how it's his fault.

"How was it was my fault?" he says, with a genuinely surprised and hurt look on his face.

This is my cue to say, "You cheated on me. Nonstop." I breath heavily and try to remain as cam as I can, try not to get too winded to run. "And no matter what your beloved mother taught you, that's a sin. A sin, Ivan. You ruined everything because you couldn't keep your dick in your pants. End of story."

"I was young, Zora. I was stupid and immature."

"From what I can tell you still are." I am so tired now, my heart racing because of the stress and the running, all I want to do is walk. But I won't show this man any weakness in me. I will keep running even if it gives me a heart attack.

He pants at my side and says in a gentle voice, "I've made mistakes. But I learn from them. You know I still love you. Zora, you are the most beautiful, brilliant, amazing woman in the world. I cry every night to think of you."

I shake my head. There's no point in arguing with him. He actually means this, what he's saying. I know he loves me. I don't think he does a very good job of it, but I know it's true. I also know that even though we're divorced and we've supposedly moved on, that when I sleep I dream I am still his wife. Somehow, my subconscious has never acknowledged the end of the marriage. In the center of my soul somewhere I still believe I am Ivan's woman, even after all he's done. I don't like to admit it, even to myself, but in the years since our divorce, I've slept with Ivan a few times, even tried to get back together in an official capacity once or twice – and he always let me down. Either he cheated again, or I would find out that I was the other woman myself; even though he'd told me he'd ended things with whatever woman he was with at the time, he hadn't.

"How's the house going?" I ask to change the subject. I slow my pace, and he matches me without saying a word. The house in question is a mansion he's building for his mother in Puerto Plata, a beautiful resort beach town in the Dominican Republic. Ivan loves his mother, Yuverkys, more than any other woman in the world, and ever since his first contract, which included a $3 million bonus (a then-record, negotiated by yours truly) he has supported her, often spending more on her than he did on his wives and children. Before that, she, a single mother, supported him by working as a cafeteria cook in the public schools. These days, Ivan earns $15 million a year and manages to spend every penny.

"You'd love it," he says.

I doubt I'd love it, but say nothing. Yuverkys is a woman with very different personal tastes from me. For instance, she thinks snarling stone lions are a good idea on a front porch.

"Does it have stone lions at the entrance?" I ask.

He jogs a little ahead of me, turns backwards and stares at me in amazement. "How'd you know that?"

I shrug.

"Mami's so happy. She's going to be able to move in next month, and she's already packing." Images of an older woman wrapping newspaper around thousands of horrible garden gnomes flashes in my mind.

"You keeping the house in Orange County for her?" I ask.

"Nah," he says. "Selling it."

"I thought you might have to move in," I say. "I mean, didn't Miss Volleyball clean you out?"

"Not really. We have a good settlement. She's been generous. Considering."

"And the nanny?"

He seems uncomfortable. "I sent her back to her parents in England."

"Pregnant?"

"She had an abortion."

I stare at him. "You're fine with that?"

"I didn't feel like it was my choice to make," he says. "Under the circumstances."

"How nice of you."

"You know how I am, Zora. You know how stupid I am."

"For once, you're right."

I don't know what it is about him, but so far, none of Ivan's wives have taken him to the cleaners in the divorces, myself included. In my case, I didn't want his money. I wanted my life and my dignity. I wanted to get away from him and heal, to raise my daughter to believe men should treat her well. But he gave me a big chunk of cash anyway, out of guilt, and gave me about ten grand a month in child support. "You made me who I am," he told me when he gave me the first check. "I owe you forever."

I took his money because he was right – I had made him who he was. But the truth is, I didn't really need that money. From that first deal I got for him, when I was only eighteen years old myself, I had clients knocking on my door for representation. I had Columbia offering me a scholarship, from undergrad through my MBA. I had an article about me in The New York Times as an agenting prodigy, the girl, they wrote, from the "hood" (how cliché) whom no one believed had the skill or guts to represent a star athlete, who "surprised us all" with her "cunning and skill." So you might say Ivan and I made each other.

I keep jogging and try not to think of Ivan's aborted baby with the nanny. I would never have had an abortion. I'm not opposed to other people doing it if they believe it's the best thing for them, but I could never do it.

Before I know it, we're at the front steps to my townhouse. I see Lissette peek out of an upstairs window with a silly smile on her face. The nanny doesn't know what she's missing out on. Children are a blessing. I feel sad for the aborted baby, and thank God for not sending me down that path. As hard as it has been to raise this child alone, it was worth it. She's a spectacular person, if somewhat too happy right now. Somewhere in her immature heart, that girl wants to see her mom and dad get back together. I have four words for her: When hell freezes over.

"So, I guess it's time for you to go." I tell Ivan. Sarcastically, I add, "Nice working out with you."

Ivan takes two tickets to the Houston Ballet out of his jeans pocket and hands them to me. "I'd hate to go alone," he says. "You know, being so macho and stupid and all that."

He might have been inconsiderate and disloyal, and he might have let his penis rule his life, but he never forgets a thing. Among many other things, I am a ballet fanatic, having once harbored dreams of becoming a dancer, and he knows it. I also managed during our marriage to cultivate his own love of the ballet, and the words he's just spoken make reference to years ago, when I mocked his reluctance to go to our first ballet together as pure, stupid machismo.

Just last week I asked my assistant to try to get me tickets for tomorrow's Houston Ballet premiere of a new Stanton Welch program, set to the music of Michael Torke. Sadly, it was sold out. I look closer at the tickets in Ivan's hands. Stanton Welch. Michael Torke. Premiere.

There must be a mole in my office. Tara's gonna hear it from me, trust me.

"Sorry, I can't," I say, hating myself as I do. I am unconvincing, and he knows it. I am practically drooling for these tickets. He smiles at my discomfort in the same way he used to smile when he'd tease me toward a climax with his mouth, only to stop at the precise moment before I exploded. He would toy with me like that for hours, until I was begging for relief.

"I can't," I say. But what I think is: Would it kill me to see the ballet with my daughter's father? As friends?

"Sure you can," he says.

I do the all-business scowl at him. He doesn't buy it, and keeps on smiling. No one in the world knows me as well as this man knows me. "I don't have time to stand here debating you, Ivan. I don't want to be late for the game."

"Ah, come on. You know you want it, baby." The way he says this implies more than the ballet tickets, and I remember with a small shudder just how amazing this man was in bed. I'm talking push-you-up-against-the-wall-and-f-your-brains-out good. I'd venture to say he is as good in bed as he is on the pitcher's mound. Then again, he's had a lot of practice. Not fair. Not fair at all.

He grins. "Oh, come on. It'll be fun."

"Maybe."

"Just say yes," he says.

I turn and walk up the steps without looking back. Then, hating myself as I do it, I turn to look at him as sternly as I can, my heart breaking all over again, and I say, stupidly, "Fine."

Mackenzie

My Aunt Rosie balances on the top step of a rickety metal ladder that is held together with duct tape. She reminds me of a golf ball. On a T. She is utterly round, wears tight white jeans with a large white sweatshirt and Birkenstock-style sandals. She wears a short, spiky, bright red wig, because lately Rosie has been experimenting with fake hair. "You get to be a certain age, you are entitled to act like a kid again," she has said by way of explaining it. She has dark blue tattoos on her arms. In other words, she is nothing at all like my mother. Rosie doesn't buy into many conventions, including, apparently, the one that says big women should not wear formfitting clothes in the color white. Sweat glistens on her thoughtful forehead as she stacks cans of Campbell's Bean with Bacon soup on the top shelf of one of the six aisles in her small corner grocery. She looks down as I walk through the front door in a jangle of bells, smiles at me and waves.

"Mackenzie!" she calls. "Whatcha got for me?"

I hold up the black portfolio notebook, feeling ridiculous about it. I don't know why she makes me do this, show her my photos all the time. It makes me feel weird. I tremble a little, still haunted by the scene at the house. I tried on the drive over here to imagine calling myself Mrs. Solis, and it sounded totally, completely wrong.

"Something wrong?" she asks.

I shake my head but Rosie just stares at me. She knows I'm lying. There's no use trying to hide anything from her.

"Dino's going to ask me to marry him," I say.

Rosie's face does not change. Most women I know, when told that Dino Solis was planning to ask me to marry him, would squeal and jump up and down at my good fortune. Rosie, though, remains blank as a golf ball in white pants.

"I saw him at my house with mom," I continue. "With a ring."

Rosie blinks once, slowly.

"They didn't know I was there."

Still she's silent.

"Rosie!" I cry. "Say something."

"I don't know what to say."

"He's a good guy. Everyone thinks he's this amazing guy. He's, like, he's going to be drafted into the NFL, and everyone is going to think he's the most amazing thing."

She doesn't speak.

"What do you think?" I ask her.

"Define 'everyone,'" she says.

"The whole country."

Rosie's lips tighten just a little, as if she's pinching back a thought. "I think you need to follow your heart."

Rosie quickly the subject. "Did you finish the photo project?" she asks with excitement. I nod and a smile erupts across her face. "Great! Can't wait to see it. Give me one second here. You'll be happy to know I finally took your advice and hired me someone to help out around here, but he's late and the cans gotta go up. Bean with bacon."

"You hired someone?"

"Business is booming," she jokes. "What can I say?"

The store, as usual, is void of customers. Rosie has never seemed bothered by that sort of thing, and always tries to help the community out, even if it means hiring someone when business is slow.

"He's new and he's already late?"

She shrugs like it doesn't bother her.

I watch her balance the cans, the tip of her tongue caught between her lips as she concentrates, and wonder whether it might be a better idea for her to put them lower. Seems like she's courting a lawsuit having something as heavy as soup cans on the top shelf. But I'm not a shopkeeper.

"Look out!" shrieks Rosie as a can tumbles out of her grip to the ground near my feet. Then again, maybe I could be a shopkeeper.

"Maybe you should put the cans lower," I say as I stoop to pick it up.

"Hand that up here," she says, ignoring my suggestion. When she looks down, her chins accordion beneath her neck, and I feel sorry for her. She is grossly overweight. You might not know it to look at her now, but Rosie was pretty once – astonishingly pretty according to the old family photos I've collected. She had smooth, fresh skin and long, straight, shiny black hair. She had a nice figure, and dark, wide-set eyes that she and my mother have in common. My grandma used to dress them alike when they were children, with crazy little dresses she made herself, and big, floppy hats or hugely fat and stretchy polyester headbands.

Last year, I scanned some of those old photos of mom and Rosie, blew them up to two feet across, and affixed them to the sides of an old console television with olive-green legs. My mother was horrified with the creation, appalled. "It's so depressing," she said. "It's like you try to bring out the worst in everything." Rosie, predictably, loved it and put it on display in her living room. Rosie thinks I'm some kind of undiscovered artistic genius. My mother wonders why I can't use my talents to come up with something pretty. There is nothing more important in the world to my mom than the concept of pretty.

"So how's the Doctor y la skinny trophy wife?" asks Rosie. She's referring to my parents.

"Okay," I say with another shrug. I don't actually know how they are. I don't ask.

"Good," says Rosie. "Give me a second."

I wander through the store. It's the same as it has been since I was a little girl. The old wooden candy case with the greenish glass top. The whirring old soda freezer against the side wall. The butcher's freezer with the two little tables nearby in the deli section. Rosie cooks all her own food for the deli, most of it Mexican food. The store always smells like masa and chile. I love it here. My mother doesn't eat Mexican food unless she has to. She prefers French food, or no food at all.

Finally, Rosie sets down the can she's holding and hurries down the ladder. "Give it," she says, holding out her hands.

I hand her the portfolio, and follow her to the front counter. She sets the portfolio down next to the plastic box for collecting pennies for the disabled, opens it, and I watch her face as she looks at the cover page.

"Our Hidden Cries," she reads. She looks at me with humor in her eyes. "Ay, tu. But you're so melodramática, Mackenzie," she jokes. "My God."

"Whatever." I glance at the clock behind the counter. I have an hour to get to Reliant Stadium. "I have to leave soon, Rosie. Hurry up."

"Pues. Leave it here with me. I'll look at it tonight."

I give her with my "no way in hell" face.

"What?" she asks. "You come get it tomorrow."

"Things tend to disappear in your world. You're not exactly organized, Rosie."

"Cómo qué I'm not organizada? I run a store, don't I?"

I look around the store. "I suppose."

"Olvidate. I'll take good care of them." She starts to flip through the photos. They're black and white images of my fellow Ranchers cheerleaders, in poses the public never sees and would probably be surprised to see. There's Brandi, falling in a streak of lights out of the pyramid in practice, a look of surprised fear on her twisted face. There's Anika, after a game, holding an ice pack to her sprained ankle, wincing in pain as her makeup drips, hers the face of a slightly-melted Barbie doll. Crystal and Deana, glaring at each other in the hallway before a game, over yet another of their imagined slights. Then there's Lisa, on the scale for the mandatory weigh-in, her chin crumpled in fear and self-loathing as Angela, our team manager and choreographer, gives her a disapproving stare. Let's just say these are not the official squad photos. Let's also say that I'd probably be very kicked off the team if anyone there ever saw them. But I can't help doing things like this, the same way a cat can't help, upon sniffing something objectionable, to claw at the ground surrounding it in an attempt to cover it up.

"Qué padre! These are incredible," says Rosie. "You make them seem so human."

"Cheerleaders are human, actually."

"You know what I mean. You give them flaws." She turns the pages slowly, inspecting each photo with a small smile. "This is good stuff."

I shrug.

"Don't do that!" She stares me down reproachfully, as she always does when I'm too self-deprecating for her tastes. "They are. You have to do something with these."

"Like what?"

She opens her eyes wide as if I've asked a stupid question. "Send them to the Chronicle."

I laugh. "Oh, yeah right. I'll just send them to the local paper. Hi. I'm no one you've ever heard of, and I have no formal training. But I'd like you to publish my photos. Please, Rosie, that's not how it works."

"Why not?"

"You can't just do that, Rosie."

"Why not?"

"The paper has a whole stable of photographers already."

She reaches across the counter and pulls out a travel book on Brazil. She shoves it toward me. "You talk a bunch of bullshit."

I take the book. "Gee, thanks, Rosie."

"Well, how else are you going to get to travel the world?"

I shrug and think about it. "If I married Dino we'd have enough money for me to travel."

Rosie shakes her head. "And if he decided to divorce you?"

"He wouldn't."

"What if you wanted to divorce him?"

I say nothing.

Rosie continues, "Mackenzie, do you know how many women in the world end up without a safety net because they put all their faith in their husband to take care of them and it didn't work out?"

"I guess."

"Or they end up trapped." She pauses and gives me a look like we both know who she is talking about, which we do. We both know she is talking about my mother. "And they stay in a place they don't like and try to make everyone else suffer because they're so unhappy."

"She's not miserable."

"A woman shouldn't ever count on a man to take care of her. You have to take care of yourself."

"I do take care of myself."

"A woman should take care of herself doing what she's passionate about."

"I'm passionate about dance and cheering."

"And you're good at it."

"Thank you."

"But you're better at this." She taps the portfolio.

"I don't know."

"What do you mean you don't know? How could you not know?"

I'm about to argue with her about my lack of skill and qualifications when a cute young man comes rushing through the front door. He wears lose, dark jeans and a ringer T-shirt, with those flat, striped kinds of sneakers all the guys are buying at Urban Outfitters. He must be about six feet tall, with a little mustache, a goatee, and funky black-rimmed eyeglasses. His wavy brown hair grows just past his ears, styled in a carefully messy adorable way. He has earrings in both earlobes. He wears a colorful backpack, and holds a green glass bottle of Pellegrino water in his hand.

"Sorry I'm late, Rosie," he says, talking in the too-fast way of very stressed-out people, as he sets down the backpack, takes out a name tag and starts to pin it to his shirt. Justin, it says. He keeps talking, "Traffic sucked. Some kind of construction crap." He notices me and looks embarrassed. "Sorry. About the cursing."

"Deep breath," Rosie tells him. She raises her arms over her head like a yoga teacher and I can see the needle marks from her insulin shots. She lowers her arms on the exhale. "In through the nose, out through the mouth."

"Houston traffic is the worst," he says. "Everyone complains about LA traffic, but I've been to LA. Even on a Saturday, man."

"Deep breath," she repeats. "Visualize waterfalls, clear blue skies, gently rolling hills. Puppies."

The young man shoots her a look of surprise, and grins. "Puppies?"

"With little bows in their hair."

"Fur," he corrects her. "Puppies don't have hair."

"Little bows in their fur."

He smiles, takes a deep breath after all, and sighs dramatically for her benefit. Rosie smiles to see he's begun to relax, then turns to me.

"Mackenzie, This is Justin. Justin, this is my niece, Mackenzie."

Justin makes nervous eye contact with me, sets his Pellegrino bottle on the counter, wipes his hand on his jeans, and holds it out to shake mine.

"Good to meet you," he says. "I've heard a lot about you."

I look at Rosie, and feel Justin's eyes slide over me, from the shiny brown ponytail high on my head, to my makeup-free face, to the slick navy-blue Ranchers cheerleader warmup suit, down to my soft white Reeboks.

"She didn't tell me a lot, I shouldn't have said that, actually," says Justin. "Not only was what I said inaccurate, it was also a total cliché, saying 'I've heard a lot about you.' Sorry."

Rosie raises a brow at me. "A man who can admit when he's wrong. Justin's an artist, like you," Rosie tells me.

"I am?" Justin seems to be only half-joking. "I thought I was a mightily oppressed, lowly grocery clerk."

"Justin is a poet," my aunt explains.

Justin shrugs at me. Rosie looks at him and then me, and raises her hands in mock despair. "What is wrong with these young people that they can't admit they've got talent?" She puts an arm around Justin's shoulders. "Justin grew up around here, and now he's in his last year at the University of Houston," she tells me, in a tone usually reserved for explaining things to small children. "On a scholarship. He's studying French and Anthropology, right, m'ijo?"

"Oui. French studies, with an emphasis on anthropology. Not nearly as manly as it sounds." He smirks sarcastically.

"He's good with languages. And he's a great writer," she continues. "He's doing music and book reviews for the Chronicle."

"One or two," he says with another apologetic shrug. To me he says, "Your aunt makes me sound like Lewis Lapham. Really, I'm just a random schmo who writes now and then."

Rosie shakes her head and clicks her tongue. "Stop being so modest," she tells him.

Outside, a vehicle starts honking in a loud, aggressive way. Long honks. Angry. I peek out the front window and see the Coke delivery truck towering over my Liberty. The driver of the truck leans out of the window and looks at the car angrily, as if his anger will make the car move on its own.

"I gotta go move my car," I tell Rosie.

She knots up her face. "Is that the Coke guy?" She cranes her neck to try to see, a look of disgust in her eyes. Rosie waves her hand in a way that tells me to relax. "Let him wait."

I look again at my car. It used to be perfectly cute, until about a month ago when I got rammed in the parking lot of the gym where I work out a couple of hours a day, by a thick-necked bodybuilder whose driving is as misdirected as his steroid use. He said it was an accident, but it happened the day I turned him down for a date. Turned out he was a Ranchers fan, and recognized me. Sometimes, you meet guys like this, men who know entirely too much about you, men with crazy, deep-set piglet-eyes like Ted Bundy's. Most of the girls on the team ignore them.

Me? I try to snap their photos when they come snorting around. I collect them. It is almost appalling how many I've taken. I'm doing a series of "books" on the side of cheerleading no one sees. The first in the series is the Hidden Cries thing I showed Rosie today. I'd like the second in the series to be these dudes. I'll call it something like "Psycho Possibly Dangerous Stupid Stalker Football Fetish Freaks." I try to take the photos so it looks like these guys are staring out of a goldfish bowl, bugging their eyes more than usual, like they're all somehow related to Steve Buscemi. That's how I see them. Anyway, the Jeep needs work. I haven't gotten around to taking it to the insurance office for the requisite photos because I've been so busy working and cheering. Besides the full-time cheerleader gig thing, practice and the games eat up about 35 hours of my time every week. Factor in my job with the dance team, and I'm lucky if I get a full eight hours of sleep at night.

"I have to go," I tell Rosie. "As much as I'd love to stay here just to piss off mister delivery man, I have a game tonight."

"Look at these," Rosie tells Justin. Did she not just hear me say I have to go? She flips through the portfolio.

"Rosie!" I cry. "I have to go."

Justin closes the book, pulls it away from Rosie, and hands it to me. Rosie snatches the portfolio back. "I'm keeping it. I'm not going to lose it. You can get it in the next couple of days."

"Fine," I say.

Honk, honk.

"Have a good game tonight," says Rosie.

"Goooo, Ranchers," says Justin, sarcastically waving imaginary pompoms in the air.

"Hey," I protest. "You got something against the team?"

"Besides the fact that the worst team in the NFL?" chimes in Rosie.

Justin shrugs disinterestedly. "Sorry, I'm not what you'd call a big 'sports' kind of guy. Me and sports. It's like gerbils and astrophysics."

I stare, dumbfounded, at him.

"I'd be the gerbil," he says helpfully. "Not the burly jock I appear to be, in other words."

What a total weirdo. A cute weirdo, though.

"True. You don't seem like a jock," says Rosie to Justin.

"What gave it away?" he asks. He flexes his nonexistent arm muscles. "The Erkel arms? The David Spade abs? The turkey neck?"

"You look okay," I tell him as I reach out to hug Rosie. Actually, Justin looks better than okay. He's beautiful, in a lithe, Johnny Depp kind of way. I've always sort of liked geeky boys like that. They're so different from most of the boys I've dated. "Bye," I tell her.

"Send those photos to the paper," she says.

"We'll see," I say.

I leave the store and avoid eye contact with the fuming Coke guy as I get into my poorly named Liberty, and drive away. I make it two blocks before my cell phone rings. I look at the caller ID. Rosie's store. What does she want now? I pick up.

"What is it, Rosie?" I ask.

Justin's voice comes next. "It's not Rosie," he says.

"Oh, sorry, I thought you were her."

"Me too. Then I looked in the mirror, and I was like, 'Rosie, what's up with the goatee, girlfriend?'"

I drive through the awkward silence for a moment, and then he says, casually as he can, "Okay, look. See. So, there's this photography show at the Houston Photography Center, about the Texas border with New Mexico, water issues, all that jive."

"Yeah…?"

"And I was hoping you'd honor me with your esteemed company."

"Are you asking me out?"

"No." I hear him breath deeply. "I mean, yes. I guess. I don't know. Am I? That's totally up to you. I mean, how you interpret this."

"I have a boyfriend."

"Yeah. The football player at UT," he says with a defeated sigh. "Rosie told me. I'm not asking you out on a date. Just, like, as a friend. That's all."

"A friend."

"Yeah. See, I'm the kind of loser who likes things like photo shows and was looking for someone to go with me. None of my friends are loser enough to go to a photography show. They're all really cool."

"You calling me a loser?" I say with a smile.

"Yeah, pretty much," he says sarcastically. "But you're nowhere near as big a loser as me. If you go with me, you'll see just exactly how big a loser I am."

I laugh. And then, against my better judgment, I agree to go to a photography show with Justin.

As a friend.

Zora

I clomp on high heels across the Ranchers' locker room at Reliant Stadium, looking for my client, all-pro tight end Reggie Pacheco. Head held high, I act like I – a fully dressed woman who has never played football and never plans to – belong here. I quickly spot him sitting on a chair by his locker, getting the kinks massaged out of his massive and muscular back by the handsome young team massage therapist. A flicker image of the two of them servicing me appears somewhere within my gray matter, and I subsume the thought, delicious as it is. God, am I ovulating, or what? Celibate for six months, and all of a sudden my head is filled with dirty pictures, most of them recurring fantasies about Ivan, who is the best lover I've ever had and, to my eye, the handsomest man to ever take breath into his lungs. Not that he doesn't have some stiff competition in the world of pro sports. Trust me, he does. Oh, yeah, girl. Excellent competition.

All around us, extraordinarily constructed men strip out of their everyday clothes and begin to get into team uniforms. Long ago I cultivated a skill for not staring at their private parts, or to at least not give the appearance of staring at the private parts, even when this is in fact what I am doing. I've expanded the territory of my peripheral vision entirely for locker room purposes. At first, in this environment, I used to be completely amazed by the variety of men's members. I was a gawker, for sure, and I came up with some pretty interesting theories. For instance, though you might assume basketball players, because of their height, would have the largest dicks, the ones I found to be best endowed were actually baseball players. I have no idea why. And it wasn't all baseball players. Just some of them, and Pedro Martinez in particular. That man was hung down nearly to his knees. It made you wonder how on earth he was able to roll it up and wear normal clothes. The ones with the smallest members overall were boxers.

"Hey, Reggie." He looks up at me with a smile, turns toward me and reaches out with his arms.

"Miss Jackson."

I hug him. Most players don't hug their agents and deliver kisses to both of their cheeks, but I'm not your everyday agent. I'm a woman, for one thing. Nonetheless, I know where a lot of these guys are from, because I'm from there, too. They feel comfortable around me. Sometimes, they feel a little too comfortable around me, and I have to remind them that it would be a huge conflict of interest for me to sleep with my clients. Not that there aren't some I'd like to have sex with. Are you kidding? We're talking professional male athletes. Imagine. There are many I'd like to do. Reggie included. But he's married, and I'm ethical, and there you go.

"How's that shoulder?" I ask. Reggie sustained a rotator cuff injury in week three of the season, but from what I can tell he's been diligent about the physical therapy.

"Totally better. You look great, Zora." He looks me up and down and I try not to mind. I suppose I courted the attention a little bit by wearing tight David Meister jeans with an equally tight black tank top and a flirty short paisley jacquard jacket, moss green, open over the top. I wore my hair down, too, and it tumbles in shiny brown waves over my shoulders. I also put on a set of Giuseppe Zanotti slides that show off the fabulous pedicure I treated myself to before I left New York.

"Thanks," I say, trying to affect a tough, deep, fast-moving voice. When I first started in this business, I consciously tried to imitate the men I spied on talking to each other at cafés and restaurants near Wall Street. I was only in high school, but I'd take the train to Manhattan, and get myself a soda in one of those places, and just sort of sit and absorb the manners and norms of business talk. I'm a good mimic. Over the years I've developed a reputation for being one of the straightest-talking, toughest, hardest-to-ruffle agents in the business, and I've never told a soul that much of it has been acting. I don't sound nearly this confident in my head, but no one needs to know that. The only person I think who does know it is Ivan.

I say, "So, listen. I'm having drinks with Bickelworth after the game tonight, and we're going to be talking about your contract extension, all the issues you and I discussed earlier this week."

"Cool," says Reggie. The massage therapist, sensing a sensitive discussion, pats Reggie on the back and tells him he'll be back in a little while. I make the mistake of looking at the therapist as he lifts his bag of toys and potions from the floor, and in the background I see a couple of male bodies, from the waist down, totally naked.

"Don't worry 'bout nothin'," I tell Reggie affecting a street tone because I know this will set him at ease. "I got your back."

Reggie gets up, letting the towel fall away from his waist. He is completely nude, and smiles at me because he knows that this is the only activity in the world where it is appropriate and acceptable to flash your agent. I know he does this to tease me, and that as a sports agent in the world of men I have to play by their rules and not be prudish or easily offended. A lot of my clients did not finish college, never went to college, or didn't understand much of what they were taught in college, being totally consumed by their craft. Otherwise, they wouldn't have been able to rise to the top of the game, so to speak. I don't hold them to lofty feminist or grammatical standards, because I understand where they're coming from. Rather, I play along with the best of them because it is in my own best interest to do so.

I let my eyes slip down his body, briefly, and flip my eyes back up to meet his. He pretends to be occupied with his deodorant.

"You take a cold shower in there?" I ask.

"No, why?"

I flit my eyes down again, then up. "Cold bath? Something. Looks like you got a little shrinkage goin' on," I say.

Reggie glances down at his boy, in truth quite respectable in size and form. "Shrinkage?"

"Cold water does that," I say. I make a pinching motion with my fingers, like a person grabbing hold of a joint. "Shrinks them right up, teensy tiny."

"I took a hot shower."

I shrug, pat him on the big, beefy shoulder, and wink. "Guess it's just bad genes then, eh?"

"Shit," he says, realizing it's a joke. Around us, a couple of the players overhear, and chuckle. They don't look at us. Overall, I think the men are just as uncomfortable with having female reporters and agents in the men's locker room as the women fundamentally are with being there.

"I'll call you after the meeting," I tell him. Reggie is readjusting the towel around his waist.

"Where you guys going? Hope he's taking you somewhere classy."

"PF Chang's," I say, rolling my eyes.

"Cheap son of a bitch," says Reggie.

"Yeah, well, not after I get through with him." I reach out to give him one last hug. "And think positive, Reggie. It could have been Mickey D's."

"Call me, but only with good news."

"No doubts."

"I mean, I don't care how late it is. I'll be up."

"Okay sweetie. Ciao."

And with that, I turn to exit the locker room, careful – but not too careful – to keep my roving eyes to themselves.

Mackenzie

I pull into the massive parking lot at Reliant Stadium, drive past the dozens of tailgate parties already underway, complete with barbeque grills, and loud stereos blaring everything from rock to country to rap. I remember coming to football games at the old Astrodome with my father and his friends when I was growing up, and sitting in the fold-out chair while dad manned the hibachi grill in the back of his big, shiny red truck, talking shop with his doctor pals while my brother played catch with other boys. Special times. I developed my love of football then. I loved the smell of the leather of the ball, the satisfying sound it made when a man caught it well. I loved the camaraderie of the fans, the easy way they all had with one another even though they could be complete strangers. There were never any complete strangers at football games, never any prejudices that couldn't be overcome by our shared love of our team, and I think that's what I liked the most, the way the whole community just seemed to totally forget their differences and problems and came together for the hours of that spellbinding game. I smile at the folks partying in the parking lot, and wave to the ones who recognize me. I don't know them, but they feel like family.

I steer to the special part of the lot reserved for players and cheerleaders and try to ignore the rumbling in my belly.

God, that barbecue smelled good. I would kill for some barbecued chicken right now, blackened but not burned, with lots of seasoning salt. I've had these totally crazy cravings for salt lately. But I know better than to binge on chicken right now, especially anything I might get from concessions here. Unless it's plain and grilled or boiled without so much as a drip of butter on it, I wouldn't be able to have it. I have a list of what I can and cannot eat any given day, courtesy of my mother. I have to follow it. I haven't eaten anything since breakfast. If I get heavier than 130 pounds, I can kiss my cheering and pageant careers goodbye. Right now, I'm nearly at my ideal weight, 120 pounds. I need to be 118 for the pageant. You wouldn't think two pounds could make much of a difference, but in the swimsuit competition, they do. Two pounds in the swimsuit competition means the difference between winning and having the judges think you look like a fat cow.

I stop at the guard gate and smile. The guard recognizes me, and waves me through with that stupid perverted smile of his. There are some men in this world that, no matter how hard you try to prove your worth as a human being, will always assume that cheerleaders are really just a fancy form of prostitute. You can see it in the way the local news media cover our cheerleading tryouts. The male anchors leer and jeer and the reporters ask us questions like we were six years old. Last year, a local reporter asked me and some of the other girls on the team to show the station's viewers a few of our secret exercises for staying so slim. Some of the girls played along, doing little dips holding on to full milk jugs to show that you don't even need serious equipment to train. It was totally and completely dishonest, in my opinion, because the truth is much grislier than what they showed the public. We don't just do a dip here and there off the edge of a chair and presto bango have a perfect little body. We have to work at it every second of every day, watch every bit of food that goes into our mouths, train a minimum of two to three hours a day, just like the players on the football team. I can't imagine a reporter for the evening news ever going up to one of the guys on the team and being, like, "Hey, could you show our viewers a few little exercises they could do at home to get a big ole body like yours?" That would be ridiculous. But the team likes for us to cultivate this image as vapid girls, pretty girls, non-threatening girls, with the main emphasis, for the public's sake, seeming always to be on how we look.

That said, I can't really blame the leering men. After all, they're only doing what they've been trained to do by everyone else. The only ones who don't seem to treat us like that with regularity are the schoolchildren. Among our many duties when we're not working our day jobs, training, practicing or performing is community service. It's one of my favorite parts of the job, actually, going out to schools or to the children's hospitals, helping to bring public awareness to important issues. That's what I'd like to do with the rest of my life, let the public know about things that they should know about but probably don't.

I look away from the slobbering, horny guard and drive on. Men like this? They actually think they can get with a girl like me. Men like that are disgusting and I hate them. Nonetheless, I wish I had my camera with me, so I could snap a shot of his lusty, droopy red eyes. I'd call it "Broken Man." I'd vow to bring one to the next game, but this is actually the last home game of the season, and I don't know for sure whether I'll make the team again next year, or if he'll be working here.

I park on the side of the lot designated for cheerleaders, pulling in at the same time as Ashley. She rolls up in her yellow Mini Cooper, still wearing her gray pinstriped suit from work. The car almost matches her hair as she exits and turns to see me getting out of my own ride.

"Hey, girl!" She trots over with a big smile on her face and gives me a hug. "You sore?" She rubs her hips. "My abductors are killing me."

"A little."

"So, how was your day?" she asks me. "Did the Beautiful Butterfly Girls get their routine perfect?"

We talk as we walk toward the locker room. I tell her about the leak in the school gym ceiling, and she is horrified.

"They can't let a school get that rundown," she says.

"I know. But the good news is I think they've got a good shot at state. What about you? How was your day?"

"You know, same old same old."

"Mechanical engineering."

"Mechanical engineering," she repeats with a smile. Ashley is smart. That's something a lot of people don't automatically think about cheerleaders, that we might be smart. Most of us are. We've got girls on the team who are lawyers, doctors, researchers, teachers. There are mothers on the team, and one of the girls has a severely autistic child who demands round the clock care from her. To look at her smiling and dancing on the field you'd never know she was going through so much at home.

Ashley and I walk toward the stadium as Molly's new black Acura slides into the lot. Ashley's face lights up in another smile and she waves. Inside the car, Molly, a pretty black woman with a long neck, waves back. We stop walking to wait for her.

"Hey, you guys!" Molly has her long auburn hair in high double ponytails and wears the same kind of team logo sweats that I'm wearing. She hurries over to us. She and Ashley greet each other with a hug and air kisses on either side of their faces. "Y'all look great," says Molly.

"You too," says Ashley.

"How was work today?" I ask Molly. She's a real estate agent by day. She grabs my hand in a jingle of gold bracelets and lets out a little squeal.

"I made a half-million dollar sale today, in cash, girl."

"Cash?" asks Ashley. We enter through the side door of the stadium, where another security guard waits. He recognizes us, and waves us past. Not quite as perverted as the last one, but close.

"Cash," repeats Molly.

"Congratulations," I say.

"You better get me a good present," says Ashley. "Diamonds would be fine."

"Yeah, right!" says Molly. "I better pay my student loans, more like."

We make our way down a long hallway. Molly opens the door to the cheerleader locker room. Our coach is already here and she greets us with a serious face. She's every bit the tough coach that the guys have out on the field, a professional dancer with a degree from a prestigious conservatory.

"Ladies," says coach Angela.

"Hello," we reply in unison.

Angela marches off to the corner reserved for wardrobe, where her assistant, is already laying out tonight's uniforms – navy blue shiny short-shorts with wide rhinestone stripes down the sides, shiny white dress/sports bras with jeweled piping, and blue arm bands with "Ranchers" in red lettering across the front. Rounding out the ensemble are red knee-high go-go boots – and shimmery red pompoms. Cute. Sexy. Really sexy. We're not supposed to talk about how sexy we feel in these outfits, because we're supposed to put out this totally wholesome American girl vibe, but the truth is, I never feel sexier than when I'm in a Ranchers uniform, out on the field, surrounded by all these talented, beautiful women.

As Ashley and I unload our duffle bags into our lockers, I tell her about Dino most likely asking me to marry him tonight.

"Get out!" she cries. I shrug. "That's fantastic!"

I smile, but feel sick. Angela mercifully appears to change the subject. She's tiny and powerful and has a total and complete Napoleon complex.

"Ladies!" shouts Angela in her chipmunk voice. "Good to see you all. Just as a reminder, we open with the Hammer jam. Then we're doing the halftime Ricky Biscayne routine, and we've got the Britney routine at the first quarter and the Aerosmith at third. Before you get dressed and head out, are there any questions or concerns about the routine?"

No one speaks. I shake my head.

"Janelle?" says Angela. "You comfortable with the stunt in the Biscayne?"

Janelle, a second-year law student at the University of Houston, nods as the humiliation of being singled out pinkens her cheeks. During practice, Janelle had struggled with the stunt, but not too badly. All of us are not only good dancers and trained gymnasts, but incredibly fast learners. We have to be. We are also versatile athletes, with strong backgrounds in dance, gymnastics and tumbling. We learn four or five very difficult routines a week, and usually with only one or two rehearsals to nail it. That stereotype of the stupid cheerleader is completely wrong. You have to be beyond smart to do what we do, with topnotch memory, and an athlete's discipline.

"Okay, then," says Angela with an enthusiastic clap of her hands. "Let's get to it! Grab your uniform, and get it goin', girls."

We stand in line and get our uniforms, then return to our lockers to change clothes. It's amazing how fit these women are. Even though you don't like to stare, you can't help but notice when someone's lost or gained a few pounds. They like to say we have no height or weight requirements, but the truth is we do. Angela lets you know it would be in your best interest to work it off. We also have skin tone requirements. Angela wants everyone to have at least a tan. I'm lucky because I'm naturally dark, but some of the paler girls have to spend a lot of time in the tanning booth, or with those spray-on tanners and lotions. The other requirement is that we have long hair. For whatever reason, football people respond better to girls with longer hair. Mine grows just past the bra-strap in the center of my back. I've only really had short hair once in my life, back when I was heavy. Mistake. Some of the girls who have a harder time growing their hair out have to use wigs or extensions for performances and photo shoots.

As we squeeze and shimmy into our uniforms, I tell Ashley about my uncertainty about Dino. "Do you think I'm crazy?" I ask.

"No, you're not crazy," she says.

"I don't know," I say.

"Look, Mackenzie. You're not crazy. You just have cold feet. It's totally normal. But you know you have to marry him, right? I mean, it's Dino Solis!"

"I know." I reach out to hug her, even though I don't really feel like it. Did she just tell me I have to marry Dino? That's not very open-minded of her. But this is not the time to talk about it.

"But if you do dump him, you send him my way, okay?"

"Circle time!" calls Angela. The girls gather together around her, and we join hands. "Dear Lord," says Angela. We lower our heads in prayer. "Please bless us tonight..."

When the prayer is over, we follow Angela out of the locker room, through the hall, to the door that will take us to the field. As we walk, I catch sight of Bill Bickelworth at the far end of the hallway, near the team offices. His voice is raised in anger. We all look over, sheepish. If there's one thing we don't like, it's an angry Bill Bickelworth. We want to make him happy the way little kids want to make their parents happy.

"Who's that chick with him?" asks Ashley.

She's talking about the woman standing with Bill Bickelworth. I gasp, because it's the same black businesswoman who bumped into me at the airport earlier in the day, the one who lost the piece of paper on the curb - the piece of paper I have in my car.

"That is so weird!" I say. I tell Ashley about the woman nearly mowing me down at the airport, and about how she dropped some papers in her rush to get into her limo but couldn't be bothered to wait for me to get them to her.

"Fate," says Ashley.

The businesswoman glances up at us as we march toward the field in a swish and rustle of pompoms, and I see the familiar look of dismissal we get from a certain kind of professional woman. She does not seem to recognize me at all. She looks us up and down as her lips close tightly. Disapprovingly.

Some of the girls have started to whisper that she is Zora Jackson, the most successful woman sports agent in the industry. I've heard of her. I've read stories on her before, a real rags-to-riches life path. That's why she looked familiar today! I think she's married to Ivan Barbosa, the sexy Dominican baseball player.

"She's gorgeous, for an agent," says Ashley.

"Yeah," I say.

"We hate her," jokes Ashley.

I break away from the squad, and approach her.

"Excuse me, miss," I say, trying to get her attention away from Bickelworth.

Zora Jackson's eyes turn toward me, burning with annoyance. I apologize and tell her about the papers she dropped at the airport, and how I saved them and have them in my car. Her look changes to one of relief and subtle embarrassment.

"You were the one chasing down my car," she says.

"You saw me?"

She nods and says, somewhat apologetically but insincerely, "I was in a bit of a rush."

"Not a problem." I am pleased to see she is at least able to acknowledge when she's made a mistake.

"I'd like to get those papers back," she says. "They're important."

"I figured."

Down the corridor, Angela barks out. "Ready, girls?"

"I have to get onto the field," I say.

Zora Jackson hands me a business card, and tells me to call her after the game, "So we can coordinate the handoff."

"Sure thing," I say, tucking the card into one of my go-go boots, lacking anywhere else to put it.

"What's your name again?" she asks.

"Mackenzie," I call out as I rush back to get in line.

"Mackenzie," she repeats, as though the name amused her somehow.

"Hurry up, de la Garza!" shouts Angela.

"Sorry, ma'am," I say.

We line up in formation, single file, pompoms on hips, and I feel my adrenaline surge. No matter how many times I've performed at a game – and I've been cheering since elementary school – I still get nervous. This, I think, is the real reason I cheer. Not to please my mother, who still believes marriage ruined her chances at a professional cheerleading career. I absolutely love the rush of anticipation. I would almost say I'm addicted to the excitement of the show.

"I said, are you ready?" Angela asks.

Shouting as one, the girls all reply: "Ready!"

Angela opens the door and the hallway is flooded with the blinding white light from inside the stadium. She counts time, and we march out, single file, pompoms rustling at our sides, chins held high, our smiles as big as they can possibly be. Sometimes, after games, my cheek muscles ache more than any other muscle in my body – from all the forced smiling.

As we high-step onto the field, a roar goes up from the crowd, and the announcer's voice booms over the loudspeakers to announce our presence. My heart begins to pound. There is no way to describe this feeling, the purity of the excitement. The stadium is absolutely beautiful, enormous and spotless, shiny and modern, with bright lights and huge viewing monitors suspended from the ceiling, with seating for more than 69,000 fans.

As we find our spots on the sidelines, right down on the field, my heart expands with pride and the thrill of this moment. The crowd roars louder with the appearance of our mascot, a cartoonish cowboy figure, who does back handsprings across the grass just behind us, ending in a roundoff.

I listen for the clicks that count off the start of the Hammer song, a corny song in just about any other context, but completely energizing here and now as the opening song for a fun night of football. It's our job to get the crowd pumped up, and I'm ready. The beats come, click, click,

click, click, and then the recognizable tune of "Can't Touch This." The crowd roars even louder, and I feel their positive energy in my bones. Then, right on cue, my body begins to move like some kind of well-oiled machine, in synch with all the others. I dance, kick, turn, flip, jump. It's hard to explain just exactly how I remember all these routines. It's almost like I don't. My body does the remembering for me and I just go along for the ride somehow. I float somewhere within my own consciousness, almost like I'm watching myself perform. It's an amazing rush.

We get to the percussive chorus of the song, all the base girls gather in formation around me and two other flyers, prepping for kewpies – stunts where the flyer-girl is held up balanced on one foot, thrown into the air and caught by the others. I'm hoisted into the air for the stunt, up toward the bright lights. I look at the faces of the fans, at the excitement and the colors, at the way the light shines. Then I see her. One woman, alone, sitting, hunched, sad, lost in thought in a sea of cheering faces. Who is she? Why is she sad? Why is she here? As I punch my hand into the air above my head, I feel the old familiar ache for my camera. My finger twitches as if it were pressing the shutter button. Snap.

She, I think, would make an awesome photograph.

Zora

The quixotic young Yardbird is ogling me with sex in his eyes, and this football game is going to end badly for the home team. No wonder I've got another killer headache coming on. I need a man, yes. But not a boy. I did that once, and look where it got me. No, thanks. If men take decades to mature, there's no way in hell I'm about to back my ass up and start over again with a college student. You crazy?

I stand up from my armchair in the lounge area of my private suite at Reliant Stadium, chug what's left of my Diet Coke, and glance around like I'm ready to go somewhere. Lissette and a female friend of hers (named something I can't remember at the moment) sit nearby, and Yardbird sits across the room, near the kitchen area, the only male in Lissette's group of friends not sitting in the box seats just beyond the lounge. He's also the only one not slurping beer and bellowing like a walrus. In fact, he seems more or less interested in only one thing, and that one thing awkwardly appears to be me. He's got him some nerve, I can tell you that. Lord have mercy. His eyes follow my every move, like a scary painting in a gratuitous horror flick. He smiles at me, locks eyes with me without shame. He is starting to creep me out, big time.

"Mom? You going?" Lissette looks up from the wedding planner she's been looking at with her little friend, who appears to have plans to marry her high school sweetheart next fall. I want to talk the girl out of it, but there's a chance it might just work out for her. Just because my marriage failed, and doomed the rest of my love life to moments like this, with a hungry, horny young man making moves on me in front of my child (does it get worse than that? I don't think so) does not mean this girl's marriage is going to fail. Maybe girls these days are smarter about whom they choose. The girls sit at the bar overlooking the seats, with a golden view of the game, but don't have interest in what's going on down on the field. They're interested in flowers, and dresses, and cakes.

"I need to get down to the locker room."

"Don't go, Zora," says Yardbird. "I was hoping we could catch some music after the game."

I look at Lissette, and then back at Yardbird. "You talking to me?" I ask him, disbelieving.

"Of course," he says. Lissette and her friend giggle. That's nice. This could not be more uncomfortable, now could it?

"Lissette, why did you bring this bombastic boy when he clearly has no interest in football?"

"He asked."

"I have interest in talking to you more, Zora," says Yardbird. "Somewhere quiet. Alone."

The girls make faces at each other in disgust. I don't blame them.

"Thank you for the overture, Yardbird, but I have other plans."

"Cancel them."

I roll my eyes at him. That boy sure has got him some nerve.

"Why don't you go romp with the other boys?" I ask. I glance past the bar, down at the young men in my seats. Their backs are to us, but I can still see them as they stuff nachos into their mouths, guzzle beer like water. Bellow. Grunt. Scratch. The usual.

"I prefer to cut loose with women," he says.

"God, Yardbird, gross!" Lissette makes a face like she wants to throw up. "Enough already."

"Like, seriously," says the little bride-to-be.

"Okay, I'm gone," I say. I grab my attache case. I ignore Yardbird and speak directly to Lissette. "I'll be home later."

"Okay, mom."

"See you soon, Zora," says Yardbird. Lissette looks at him like his obvious interest in me totally disgusts her. I want to ask her what the big deal is, because at some level I am very flattered by the handsome young man's interest.

But I know she's right. It is pretty gross to have your college buddy drooling over your mom in front of you. Gross, and not right.

As I take the elevator down to the locker room I strategize. There has to be a good way for me to get Reggie more money. The whole game is very much like chess, being an agent. Knowing your opponent's delicate points. Bluffing. The losing streak this team has been on is not going to strengthen my position. Not at all. I'd be in such a better position if they were winning, and specifically if Reggie himself were contributing to the team, which he most certainly is not. He's having one of his worst seasons, statistically. Not. Good.

I exit the elevator just in time to collide with a gaggle of sweaty Ranchers cheerleaders prancing back in from the field, trying not to look defeated and annoyed at the lousy game. I remember the one with my contract pages, and hope she remembers to call me. I search for her, but don't see her. The others bother me, just by existing. Nothing is more annoying to me than women who pretend to be happy when they aren't. You see a lot of this in professional cheerleaders. They're like Stepford wives in bikinis that pretend to be shorts. I stand and gawk at them. I know I shouldn't, but there's the whole girly thing where you check out other women to make sure you measure up, or to lament the fact that you don't. With this particular crowd, I'd bet on the latter for myself.

A couple of them smile at me, but mostly they try to act like I'm not there at all. I suck in my gut as an instinct. What is that shit? I think. Competitive instinct? Come on, Zora, you know better. I couldn't compete with these little tight-bodied girls no matter what I did. Please, girl. I'm a mother, in her thirties. I would not stand a chance. The very sight of them reminds me of the way Ivan always stared at beautiful women in front of me, like I wasn't even there, slobbery as a hound, and this reminds me of the way he actually did a lot more than stare at women. He slept with them. I stare at these women and realize that I hate them for the fact that Ivan would find them attractive. This is an unhealthy response. I should be hurrying to meet Reggie, but I'm standing here looking at a bunch of women I hate because I think my ex-husband would want to fuck them. There is something wrong with me. I honestly believe I am starting to lose my mind.

As they file past, I wonder – and not for the first time – what drives grown women to do this job. They get paid shit – about sixty-five dollars a game, compared to the nearly one million bucks a football player might make for a game. I've heard that there are some teams in the NFL that don't pay their cheerleaders at all, but give them a couple of tickets to the game for compensation. Professional cheerleaders don't get much respect, either. Then again, most women who prance around in short-shorts and halter tops with thigh-high boots don't tend to get a lot of respect to begin with. Attention, yes. But not the kind of attention I'd personally like to get as a woman. They get a little bit of respect among their peers, from other cheerleaders, but not much from anyone else. Not as much as, say, women in power suits and heels. Then again, I think every woman would secretly love to have the kind of body that would allow us to prance around in short shorts and halter tops in public, even if we would never admit it to anyone we knew. I think most of us wouldn't mind too much trading in respect for attention – like hardcore drool-mouthed male attention – now and then. But to do it all the damn time? Please, girl. You'd have to be half crazy out your damn mind.

I don't mean to imply I don't appreciate their skill. From a simple athletic standpoint, these women are as serious about their craft as the men on the field. But I can't stand the way the football culture pretends they're these "wholesome" girls when in fact they are paraded around like women who might be porn stars if they weren't so Christian or something. It's sick. Almost as sick as me standing here staring down a bunch of strange women and feeling lost and insecure – and old as hell – among their sinew and cleavage.

I turn away from the cheerleaders and head toward the men's locker room.

"Uhm, Mrs. Jackson?"

I turn around and see the cheerleader from the airport, trotting after me with a big smile on her face. It looks painful to smile like that.

"Yeah?"

"I'm sorry. I don't mean to keep you. Or to be rude. The card you gave me, it fell out somewhere on the field."

I nod, and hand her another card.

"Wow," she says, still smiling as she looks at the card. Her teeth are very white and very straight. She's a beautiful woman, but seems a little immature or unguarded, a little too enthusiastic. Me, as you know, I'm all about the walls. People without boundaries scare me. She holds her hand out for me to shake it. "My full name is Mackenzie de la Garza. This is my third year cheering for the Ranchers, and I just wanted to say I think you're amazing."

"Thank you," I say. I try to turn to leave, but she keeps talking. Great. Another one of those people who never knows when to end a conversation. It's a boundaries thing. It has to be.

"Some of the girls said you have a daughter who goes to Rice. I went there, too! I was just wondering, and this is going to seem like a really weird question probably, but I was just wondering how you managed to get where you are in business and everything while juggling motherhood and a husband?"

I laugh out loud. "No husband, child," I say.

"Oh, I'm sorry. I got that wrong. I'm sorry. I mean, juggling a child. I guess that's what I mean."

I look into her eyes. I mean really look into them. They are a very dark shade of brown, almost black – large, wet eyes that because of the darkness of the iris seem all pupil, like they might be able to see in the dark. Smart eyes. There's a lot more there than you might first assume. I smile back at her. "No," I say. "I mean 'no husband' is the reason I was able to get so far."

"Really?" Girl seems cold stone shocked.

I consider it. "Yes," I say. "Really. I don't think I could have focused as hard as I did if I was always worried about getting some man's approval. At the time it seemed hard, but now that I look back on it I think it was a bit of a blessing."

Mackenzie de la Garza, the cheerleader, nods her head as if understanding something for the first time. "Can I ask you something else?"

"Yeah, but make it quick. I have a meeting and I'm going to be late as it is."

"Oh, sorry! It's not a big question. Just, where did you get that jacket? It's so pretty. I love it."

"Thanks." I look down at the blazer and try to remember. "Neimans," I say. "Neiman Marcus."

"My mom shops there all the time," she says. And then seeing that this comment is more than a little offensive to me, she backtracks. "No, I didn't mean it like that, I just meant that, it seemed like you didn't think I'd know where that was, or what it was, but I totally almost practically grew up there, shopping with my mom. And me too, don't get me wrong. I've gotten plenty of things there. I just loved your jacket, I think it looks great on you and I totally wasn't trying to say you dress like my mother."

"I gotta go," I say. First Yardbird, now this shit. What a day. I crave Tylenol like a junkie craves smack.

"Of course. I'm so sorry. Don't be late. Go. Thanks for talking to me." She blushes a little bit, and bites her bottom lip a little bit with a tiny little smile and an almost too-direct, borderline improper look in my eyes. I want to look away, but don't do it quick enough. She seems to giggle a little bit, and plays with a piece of her hair, still looking at me. If I'm not mistaken, this is the kind of body language women use when they're…flirting.

No way.

"I need those papers," I say.

"I know. I can get them to you tonight, if you want."

"Call me in a bit. I'm late."

I turn and walk quickly away, quite sure that I've mistaken a friendly cheerleader's interest in my jacket for sexual interest in me personally. This is what I mean when I say I need a man in my life, and if not in my life at the very least in my bed. I'm starting to imagine all kinds of crazy shit. They used to say that self-pleasure made you go blind and crazy, and now, after six months of that secretive shit, after hallucinating that a super hot Ranchers cheerleader, sweaty and half-naked, just came on to me in the bowels of Reliant Stadium, I'd have to say I'm starting to agree. Maybe I need more than a man. Maybe I need a shrink.

Mackenzie

No husband. That's how she did it.

No husband.

You see? You don't have to get married to have a good and happy life. You don't even have to have a husband to raise a pretty normal and well-adjusted kid, or at least a kid who gets into Rice. Zora Jackson made her way without a man.

I am alarmed by how right that sounds to me. I'm supposed to want a husband. I can't think of a time in my life where it was ever not assumed by everyone around me that I would grow up, get married and have children. There was the whole thing with Barbie and Ken, that's when it started. No, wait. It started totally way before that. It started with the dolls and the little pretend kitchen I used to have, and with the way the boy down the street would come over and we'd play house, and house meant a husband and a wife. House never meant, like, me living there all by myself with a darkroom and maybe a dog or something, and the boy down the street coming over to have sex now and then. And you know what? It absolutely should have been an option to play it that way, only without the sex part because we were only really little kids. We should have totally been allowed to play house where I lived alone with a darkroom and was famous for taking photographs and the boy down the street could have been like this mysterious writer type of dude who came over now and then to make dinner for me and he'd wear nothing but his boxer shorts and an apron. Oh, wait, I'm back to the whole sex part. But you know what I mean. It should have been okay for a little girl to play house by herself. That's what I'm trying to say.

Marriage. It is what I've been raised for. It's what most girls I know have been raised for. But the more I think about it – and ever since seeing Dino with that ring on my mom's sofa I've had nothing else to think about – I just don't honestly think I want a husband. Not yet. Not now. I like my time to myself. I like not having to answer to anyone or argue with anyone. I love kids, but I don't know if I could ever see myself having kids of my own.

I can't believe I'm having these thoughts. You have no idea what my mother would do to me if she knew I was having these thoughts. She'd start by crying until snot ran out of her nose because that would let me know I'd ruined her life. Then she'd move to throwing me out of the house. I don't know why I think she'd do that, but I totally do, like if I'm not going to be a good little breeder daughter for her then there's not even a point in having a daughter. I don't know why, if a woman is able to take care of herself, she can't just have a boyfriend or something and leave it at that.

I'm walking across the parking lot toward the PF Chang's on Westheimer Road, which I managed to persuade Dino to meet me at (and which I wanted to go to because I knew Zora Jackson would be there) when my cell phone rings. I check the caller ID. It's my mom.

"Hello?"

"Mackenzie," she says, more accusation than greeting. I can hear the TV blaring in the background, and my father scolding one of mom's little dogs. My father is a cat person. My mother loves dogs. That sums up their marriage. "I just wanted to remind you to be a perfect little lady tonight with Dino."

"Mom–"

"He's a good man, Mackenzie."

"And?"

"And you're incredibly lucky. Just remember that."

I say nothing, because all of the things I want to say would be considered impolite.

"So behave yourself. None of this talk about running off to the Amazon to take pictures of starving babies. Por el amor de Dios."

"Who told you about that?" I ask.

"Rosie called today."

"What did she say?"

"Nothing. Forget I brought it up, honey. I think you're spending too much time with her."

"Well, even if I did want to be a photojournalist would it be the worst thing in the world?"

"Yes."

"Rosie thinks I'm good."

"Is that what you want, to end up fat, alone and broke like Rosie? Wearing a different wig for every day of the week?"

"Mom, enough." I am getting upset.

"Watch your attitude," she hisses. "Or you'll end up losing another perfectly good man, and the chance to have a very happy, comfortable life. He's a good catch, Mackenzie. A great catch."

I realize she's probably right, and then I realize that this was her goal – me realizing she was right. That has always been my mother's goal. "I'll see you later."

"Bye, sweetie." She sounds positively giddy. "Good luck."

I hang up. Just as I'm about to open the door, my cell rings again. It's mom. I fight the urge to throw the phone on the ground.

"Hello?"

"I forgot. Don't talk too much. Sometimes you have a tendency," says my mother.

"A tendency?"

She explains, "Of talking too much. Here's a secret about men. A man never wants to feel like a woman is smarter than he is. I mean, we know we're smarter, but the smart thing to do is to let the man think he's smarter. That way you get what you want out of them."

"Bye, mom. Oh, and 1950 called. They want their values back."

"Not funny."

"I have to go."

"I love you. Make me proud. This is a very important night."

"Yeah? How come?"

"Try to come home early. I'll wait up for you."

"Why?" I ask, though I already know why.

"We'll want to talk. See you later. I love you."

"Bye."

I hang up, walk into the crowded lobby of PF Chang's, and peer through the throng of bodies in search of Dino. I've got my digital camera in my purse, and resist the urge to yank it out. The faces, the lighting, it would make an interesting, reddish photo. I live for unexpected great photo moments like these. But I'm already ten minutes late, and don't want to be rude.

"Mackenzie!"

I turn to see Dino standing near the hostess stand, waving. I wave back, and we move toward each other through the crowd. I feel eyes on us. It's got to be hard for most women not to stare at Dino. Personally, I never had any success at not staring at him. At six-foot-three, he's tall.

He has a beautiful body, a very fit quarterback's body, solid and super strong. His face is pretty enough to have landed him a male modeling contract with the Ford agency, and he's found himself already fielding calls from companies like Nike about possible endorsement deals – though he cannot sign a deal until he's out of college, of course.

"Hey, baby," he says as we come together. He draws me into a big old bear hug, and I breathe in his scent. Dino and I have alarmingly good body chemistry together. "You look beautiful."

"You look awesome, too," I say.

As we move out of the hug he slips his hand discreetly around my side and underneath one of my breasts, just brushing it.

"Hey," I say, offended. He has a playful smile.

"Sorry. You're just so fuckin' hot," he says. It smells like he might have gotten here a little early and hit the bar without me.

Behind us, a couple of people mutter Dino's name, as in, "Hey, isn't that Dino Solis?" Sure enough, a couple of middle-aged white men in khakis come up to us – just in time to see him cop another feel – and ask him if he's Dino. He smiles and nods. They shake his hand vigorously and ask for his autograph on scraps of paper and a newspaper. He obliges, and then says, "Gentlemen, if you'll excuse me,

I have a date with this beautiful little lady and I'd like to get to it."

"Mister Superstar," I tease.

"I've already got a table for us," he tells me with a wink and a grin. He takes my hand gently and leads me through the crowd. I'm amazed by how many people stare at him. Amazed, yet not surprised. Football is a religion in Texas, and lately Dino is the high priest. I feel proud to be with him, and almost feel bad that I am prouder to be with him than I was to be cheering for the losing Ranchers tonight.

Dino leads me to a quiet booth toward the back of the restaurant. There is a vase with a dozen red roses on the table. I gasp. Dino grins.

"They're so pretty," I say.

He stands and guides me into the booth, gently tweaking my bottom as I pass him.

"Dino!" I protest.

He lowers his voice and says, "I'm sorry, baby, it's just you look so amazing I wanna bang you right now, on the table."

"Dino, please," I say, hoping my annoyed facial expression will tell him I prefer he keep his filthy thoughts silent right now.

"Sorry. You're just like the hottest woman I ever saw. You make me crazy."

"How was your day?" I ask him, sitting and placing the napkin in my lap – partly for manners' sake and partly as a Dino-shield. I've had sex with Dino - though my mother thinks we're waiting - and I'm sorry to say it was quick and to the point. His point, not mine. I'm in no rush to do it again, honestly.

Before he has a chance to answer, the waiter glides over and tells us about the various sauces and ways to order. I love this restaurant, and I'm starving. I don't bother to look at the menu. Even though Dino is something like fifth or sixth generation Mexican American, and a native of Houston, he still has a few little machista tendencies, like ordering for me and opening every door in sight for every woman around.

"Do you need a few more minutes to decide?" the waiter asks.

"No, actually. We're ready to order," says Dino.

The waiter takes out a pad and a pen. "Before I take your order," he says sheepishly, "would you mind signing this for me? My dad would die if I brought home Dino Solis' autograph."

"Sure," says Dino, clearly enjoying the attention.

"So, you think you'll be number one in the draft?"

"It's lookin' that way, man," he says, handing the signed pad back to the waiter.

"Think you'll come to Houston? I mean, they'll get first draft pick as shit as they've been playing lately, and you know they're gonna want you, the homeboy."

"I can't divorgenate about this," says Dino, rolling in his new celebrity like a pig in mud. Divorginate? What the hell is he talking about? That's not even a word.

Dino keeps talking, and my head keeps starting to hurt: "But I appreciate the kind words, dog."

The waiter returns to his actual job now, but still looks star struck. "Okay, so what'll you have?"

"We'd like to start with the spare ribs and an order of the calamari," says Dino.

I'm not big on ribs, and I detest calamari. Dino continues ordering.

"Then we'll take a cup of wonton soup each. Give us the lo mein pork, almond cashew chicken and a bowl of the steamed white rice."

"That all?"

"And a bottle of wine."

"Any particular one?"

"Something white, I guess."

Even though I am something of a wine expert, thanks to my Aunt Rosie's great palate and education of me, he doesn't ask my opinion or look for me to advise him.

"Okay. Be right out."

As the waiter leaves, Dino leans back in his seat, gloating, with a self-satisfied smirk. "Can you believe all the people just coming up to me? I'm famous, girl."

"How does it feel to have all this attention?" I ask.

"Great. I always knew it'd happen."

"Really?"

"Sounds crazy, but I did. I always kind of knew." He leans forward and lowers his voice a little. "And how does it feel for you? I mean, it must be pretty amazing to have me for a boyfriend right now."

It takes me a moment to answer because I am stunned by the arrogance of what he's said. I smile my best cheerleader's smile. "I'm proud of you, Dino."

His eyes wander across the crowd, almost as if he's in search of more attention, and suddenly his jaw drops open. "I can't believe who's here. Look."

I turn as casually as I can manage and look across the room. I'm pretty sure I know who it's going to be. Bill Bickelworth. Zora told me she was having a meeting with him here tonight, when I called her after the game. That's why I managed to get Dino to change our plans and bring me here. I've got her papers in my handbag. Bickelworth is walking across the restaurant with Zora. He's a tall, paunchy man, his face ruddy and flushed, as if he's been drinking or arguing, and he wears a three-piece suit.

Usually when I see him he's in a polo shirt and khakis, or a team sweatshirt.

"It's fate," says Dino, who has never met Bickelworth but keeps hounding me to introduce him. It's one of the many things Dino seems to have to talk to my dad about. Both of them think I'm stingy because I haven't invited the man to dinner at our house or something, but the truth is I don't really feel like I know him well enough to introduce anyone to him. I mean, I see him at every game, but he's got this way of looking right through the cheerleaders that makes me think he wouldn't have a clue who I was if he met me out of context and uniform. This might prove to be the night I put that theory to the test.

"He looks busy," I say. The waiter comes and pours a little bit of wine into Dino's glass. Dino has no idea that the waiter is waiting for him to sample the wine and approve it. I catch the waiter's eye, and motion for him to go ahead and fill the glasses for us.

"Sorry," I mouth to the waiter. It crosses my mind that if I do in fact marry this man, I am going to spend an awful lot of my life apologizing for him.

"Who's that hottie with Bick?" asks Dino. I don't think he knows the coach well enough to use diminutive names with him, but it's not my place to say so.

"That's Zora Jackson, the famous sports agent."

"She's way hot," he says. "You think it's a date?"

"He's married," I remind Dino. "I'm sure it's all business. She's all business. I saw her at the game earlier. She's got incredible confidence. Sometimes I wish I could be more like that."

Dino shrugs as if that wouldn't matter, and I feel ice in my veins.

"I think you're fine the way you are," he says.

"But I mean it would be amazing to be able to talk to anyone the way she does. She's totally not afraid of anything."

"You don't need to be like that."

"But I think I want to."

"You want to be a ball breaker? Come one, Mackenzie. You're perfect as you are."

"You don't understand," I say, pouty. He rolls his eyes.

"God, Mackenzie, just calm down, okay?"

"I am calm." I sip the wine and hope that it will soon take away the uneasy feeling I have in my gut. It's more than just hunger. It's dread. I can't look at Dino. Where last week I was perfectly content with our relationship, I feel like running away now that I know what's coming.

"What?" he asks. "You jealous because I said that woman's hot?" He downs his entire glass of wine in one swallow, wipes his mouth on his sleeve.

"I'm not jealous."

"It doesn't mean I'm gonna go screw her," he says. "Jesus, ease up."

"Yeah, okay," I say. This whole thing sounds so much like my parents I want to cry. I don't want a marriage like that. I really don't.

Dino is trying not to stare at Bickelworth. I notice that everyone in the restaurant has noticed that there are two football stars in our corner, and they've begun to whisper. I try not to stare at Zora but my ears are definitely trained in her direction. She's extremely attractive, and I'm more fascinated than jealous. Most of the beautiful women I've known try not to be too intimidating, or too smart. They try, like Texan geishas, to make men comfortable. This woman looks like she could care less whether men around her feel comfortable. I listen hard to what she's saying.

"If you think I'm going to agree to that shit, you're crazier than I thought," I hear her say. My heart practically stops in my chest. Not only does Zora walk with supreme grace and confidence, but she's cursing at and insulting Bill Bickelworth.

Dino gets distracted by a blonde woman with huge boobs who comes giggling over to ask him for his autograph. I hate her, and I hate the way he's looking at her. I try to ignore them, and listen instead to the woman at the next table.

"Reggie's the best player you've got," Zora says. "So the way I see it, you really don't have a choice. You can give him what he wants, or you can lose him to Seattle, Pittsburgh, or Green Bay after the season – all of which have room under the salary cap to pay more than you're willing to."

Next to me, Dino is shaking the woman's hand a little too long. I know that professional athletes have this affect on a certain kind of woman. I see it all the time. There are so many groupies after the Ranchers, you wouldn't believe it.

Bickelworth chews from the appetizer that has already arrived at his table. We're still waiting for ours. He swigs from a frosted glass of beer, narrows his eyes at the woman and points his finger at her. "Reggie's too cosmopolitan to want to live in those places. Green Bay? We're talking about one of the most educated players in the league here. He goes to the fucking symphony, Reggie. And his house over in River Oaks? Have you seen that monster? Jesus. Had it built from scratch, his wife's dream home."

I realize now that they are talking about Reggie Pacheco, the all-pro tight-end for the Ranchers, who is about to become a free agent after this season. She must be his agent.

Zora looks amused by Bickelworth's defense, and counters. "Reggie's concerns transcend entertainment, Bill.

Last I checked, Seattle had a serviceable symphony. Don't insult me. Besides, he told me about this nice house outside of Pittsburgh, with a great school for his girls."

"Quit staring," says Dino.

"Sorry," I say.

"So, you asked me how my day was, before all this," he says. "And I didn't get a chance to answer. I had a good day."

"I'm glad."

We sit in silence as Dino pours more wine and guzzles it. "This is sick," he says, looking around the room with a smile. "People know my name."

"Yeah," I say. I guzzle my own wine. "I had a tough day," I say.

"Yeah?" Dino drinks and watches the woman with the big boobs. Usually I'd tell him about why the day was good or bad, but right now I just don't have the energy to try to interest someone who is so clearly not interested in me and the moment.

I glance over at Zora and Bickelworth again, and see him staring at Dino. Zora catches my eye, and nods toward me, noting Dino as well, with a look of surprise to see me with him. Pleasant surprise. Bickelworth looks at me briefly, and I smile and wave, hoping he'll realize who I am. His face registers no recognition, but he offers a weak smile in return.

"So, basically we need you to show how much you want Reggie to wear a Ranchers jersey next season," Zora says. I look at Dino to see if he's listening, but he's not. He's smiling at the blonde woman from earlier. "God knows the Ranchers need a marquee player, Bill. I mean, it's pretty sad you guys can't fill seats in Houston anymore. Houston, Bill. Football capital of the world, and it's like a ghost town in the stadium."

I hardly notice when our waiter sets the appetizers on our table. Dino starts in with his hands. "You gotta try these," he says of the ribs. "God." Gingerly, I pick up a rib and nibble at it. It's not half bad, but there's something sick about the thought of eating a creature's ribs.

Bickelworth watches Dino eat, and turns his eyes back to Zora. "Yes, we suck at the moment. Everyone knows that. You're not covering any new ground here, Zora. But the kids look up to Reggie. Especially the Latino kids, especially with his foundation. Houston's a Hispanic city now, you know that. What would all those kids and their families think if they found out Reggie Pacheco, son of migrant workers like some Grapes of Wrath character, left his home state to go to fucking Wisconsin? He'll lose fans. No one's gonna love that boy in this town anymore. Especially not if there's another hot young Latin player coming in as a superstar. And none of the cities you named for me have much of a Latin population."

His eyes move back to Dino just in time to see my charming boyfriend shove a rib into his mouth. Bickelworth laughs, and stands up. "Come with me a second," he says to Zora.

"What?"

"Just come here."

She gets up, and follows him a few steps to our table. Dino drops the rib on his plate and wipes his hands, a grin spreading across his face.

"Dino Solis?" asks Bickelworth.

Dino jumps to his feet, and extends a hand. "Mister Bickelworth, what an honor."

"Likewise, son. A helluva season you've had so far. To bad about the Heisman, though."

I watch Zora's face. No sign of emotion. A poker face. If she has any idea how famous Dino is, or what a good shot Houston has of getting him to play for the Ranchers next year, she doesn't show it.

"Zora, I'd like to introduce you to Dino Solis, the man who won the Fiesta Bowl for Texas last year and he's headed for the BCS title game this year."

She shakes Dino's hand. So far, everyone has ignored me. I can't even tell if Zora recognizes me from earlier. Granted, I was wearing a lot less then, and was sweaty. "Hello, Dino," says Zora. "Pleasure to meet you."

"Well," says Bickelworth. "Just wanted to say hello, introduce myself." He smiles triumphantly.

"I appreciate that, sir," says Dino.

"Texas is proud of you, son."

"Thank you, sir."

Zora turns her attention to me, and she smiles in a nicer way than she has yet, presumably because she knows I know Dino. My heart falls. This, I think, is what it will be like for the rest of my life with this man; being appreciated because I belong to him. Her eyes shock me with their intelligence and directness. I am envious. I am hit with the realization that I want to be just like her when I grow up, and then I realize I am already twenty-three and ought to grow up soon. But I can't imagine ever having that kind of confidence.

"Hi," she says, extending her arm. "I think we met earlier. Mackenzie, right?"

I shake her hand. "Yes, ma'am," I say.

Bickelworth looks at me at last. I smile at him, and say, "I don't know if you recognize me, sir, but I'm a cheerleader for the Ranchers." And, I add silently, I have been for the past three years.

Bickelworth looks embarrassed as Zora smirks at him in a smug way that tells me I just inadvertently gave her ammunition to use against him. He did not recognize me, and he knows that we all know it.

"Of course," he says. "How are you, Casey?"

"Mackenzie," corrects Zora, with a wink at Bickelworth. "Good Texan name. Mackenzie de la Garza. Hard to forget, Bick. I'm surprised."

I answer him, "Fine. Tired, but fine."

"You girls cheered hard tonight. You have a right to be tired."

"I have your stuff," I tell Zora. I can tell by her harsh look that it was a mistake. She shakes her head almost imperceptibly.

"Good to meet you all," she says, somewhat uncomfortably.

"Enjoy the rest of your dinner, folks," says Bickelworth, as he pulls Zora back toward their own booth. She looks over her shoulder at me and motions for me to meet her in the bathroom, then points to her watch and mouths "five minutes".

Dino looks on as Zora slides back to her seat at the table with Bickelworth.

"Zora Jackson," he says with a narcissistic smile. "I read a story on her in ESPN magazine where it said she makes more than ten million a year in commissions alone. Her company is worth about a hundred million."

And she didn't have to get married to do it, I think.

Five minutes later, Zora heads to the ladies' room, and I excuse myself to follow. She's standing at the sink reapplying lipstick when I walk in.

"Not too much talking," she tells me, looking at me in the mirror. "Didn't realize you were attached to Dino. Doesn't look good to have me getting papers from you, NCAA rules and all."

"I understand, Miss Jackson," I tell her, as I dig through my bag for the three sheets of paper. I smooth them out and hand the to her.

"Thank you," she snaps, turning to snatch them from my hand and quickly stowing them in her attache case. She walks from the room with only a quick, hard smile for a goodbye, and I feel sad that I might never get a chance to talk to her again. There are so many things I'd like to ask her.

I freshen up my own makeup, adjust my hair a bit, and return to the dining area, to Dino and the food I didn't order.

An hour later, after we've had dinner and desert, and after Bickelworth and Zora Jackson have left the restaurant joking jovially with one another – he still liked her even after the way she treated him! – Dino produces the ring box, his cheeks red with wine and excitement. He opens the box. It's a lovely ring. Really. A beautiful ring, expensive. He looks up at me. "So, will you marry me or not?"

It's a lovely ring. So round, so shiny, with such a big diamond. Probably cost him $10,000.

"I don't know," I say.

Dino's is stunned, as if he's just been sacked by the opposing defense. "You don't know?"

"I'm sorry, Dino, I just don't think I'm ready. I'm only twenty-three."

He closes the box and quickly shoves it back into his jacket pocket. He looks around self-consciously, hoping no one has just witnessed me rejecting him. "You're crazy," he tells me. "Only twenty-three, yeah, but just how many times do you think you're going to get pro-sitioned by a guy who's probably going to get a contract worth 80 million dollars? Women are lining up to be with me."

Prositioned? That's not even a word. I cringe, and try to imagine a lifetime of listening to made-up words.

"Like I said, I'm very proud of you. I'm honored you'd ask me. And someday, I'd really like to marry you. I just don't think I'm ready."

"My God!" He laughs like he can't believe any of this. "Do you have any idea how many women would die to be in your shoes right now?"

"I know, but-"

"Do you have any idea how pissed off your family will be when they find out you rejected me? Your mom and dad love me. They think this is a great idea, me and you."

"I didn't reject you, Dino. I just asked you to hold off for a while."

Dino laughs like he doesn't care. "It's now or never, Mackenzie," he says. "We've been together for a whole year. I love you."

I star at my empty wine glass, and think. He's right. I know he's right. "I love you, too," I say.

"So what's the problem?"

"There's no problem," I say. "I'm just afraid to give up my life."

"Who says you'd have to do that?" He slips a hand over mine. "You can keep doing everything you're doing. The pageants, the cheering. I don't expect you to quit everything and have babies right away or nothin' like that."

"You don't?"

"No!" He looks surprised I'd even think this of him. "I just want you, girl. The waiting is killing me."

"But you have me."

"I want more than that. I want us to live together. I want us to be a family. I'm crazy about you. I've never been this crazy about a chick in all my life."

"But you don't know everything about me."

He squeezes my hand and looks into my eyes. "I know enough."

"What if there were some things about me you'd hate, Dino?"

"My love for you would be big enough to get over it. Unless you like killed someone or something."

My heart sinks. "Yeah," I say.

"So what do you say? I'll give you all the space you need to have your own life. You can keep everything the way it's been, only now you'll have an ally in your life, someone to support you and stand by you. That's all I want."

I look into his beautiful brown eyes, and realize how foolish I've been. I smile.

"Okay."

"Okay?"

"Okay. Yes. I mean yes, Dino, I'll marry you."

I know as I say it that I don't entirely mean it, but I justify the lie by telling myself it will be easier to get out of this some other time. I'm not good at hurting people's feelings.

Zora

I weave my fast little silver Mercedes CL55 AMG in and out of traffic on Interstate 10, on my way back to the townhouse. I'm driving too fast. I know this. I'm doing about 95 miles per hour. But I can't help it. I'm feeling a little out of control.

The car, my Houston car, was actually a gift from a very famous Chinese basketball player I helped negotiate one of the biggest contracts in the sport this year. He is polite, and shows his gratitude mightily – the car cost him more than $120,000. This is why Lissette is not allowed to drive it, even though the car sits in the garage doing nothing while I'm in New York. I'm anal enough to check the mileage when I come into town. Lissette's good about following the rules – not at all like me when I was her age. Then again, it's not like she's starved for a nice car of her own. Her father bought her a silver convertible Audi for her high school graduation last year.

My car, however, has 493 horsepower and a supercharged V-8, which partially explains why I'm driving so damn fast; the other reason is that prick Bill Bickelworth. I'm sick of dealing with him. He's got a losing team, and his best years are behind him, but he hasn't figured out yet what a has-been he is and no one in this polite-ass town seems to have the balls to tell him. Not even that dopey little cheerleader whose name he didn't know and then couldn't remember after she had (quite politely, I may add) told him. Casey? No, he didn't. Did he? Did he actually call her Casey? My God. I wonder if she has any idea how handy she was for me tonight in getting Bick off balance. She must know. Or maybe not. Hard to tell. I do think it's very strange that after talking to me in the hall at the stadium and giving me that look, that crazy little flirty look – and no, I do not think I was imagining that shit – this woman shows up at the same restaurant. That was a little unusual. I know I must have mentioned it sometime. Did she hear me? Did she follow me? Houston is a big-ass city, okay? We're talking fourth-largest city in the country. That we would all just happen to end up in the same damn place. Uh huh.

I'm losing my damn mind, that's what's happening here. I'm overworked and hallucinating. I need a vacation. A nice, long, relaxing vacation. But here's the sorry truth. I have never, not once in my damn life, had a vacation. Not since I started working, and I started working in high school, okay? High school. I have not taken a vacation since I was a little girl with my parents, and even then it wasn't much of a vacation, just a trip now and then to Chicago or Mississippi, so that some relative I'd never heard of could talk about how I better keep my pants up when I got to be grown. Ivan and I took some trips, and I traveled with him and Lissette a lot, but I never let myself relax. I have been running since I put my own feet on the ground, with this intense sense of urgency that I still carry, like if I don't keep on keeping on, doing the thing I do, on and on forever and at as fast a pace as I can, that the whole damn thing might just be a dream that disappears all around me and I'll just end up back in the South Bronx projects. I don't want that. I do not, let me repeat that – I do not – I do not ever want this good thing to end, the money and the power. And I'm just crazy and insecure enough to think deep down that if I ever stopped to catch my breath I'd end up losing the race altogether. That's why nights like this make me so jumpy. That's why I'm driving so fast. I can't stop, I can't slow down. I can't look back. I have to charge ahead and find a way out of this, to solve this problem.

I left the restaurant empty-handed, which isn't usually the way I do business. I should have gotten my papers from Mackenzie, too, but I didn't want Bickelworth misinterpreting it as me trying to make a move on Dino Solis before he was out of school. I was all thrown off my game. Bickelworth is a notorious sexist, so it didn't surprise me the evening was so difficult. I've never had a smooth time dealing with him. But he's never made it this hard, either. And to get up and act like Dino Solis is actually going to go to Houston? No one even knows if the kid is going to be the first draft pick. That's all media talk, and what the hell do those suckers know about anything? But, you know, if he is I certainly hope he calls me. I'd like nothing more than to negotiate with Bickelworth for Solis, especially after Bickelworth drives Reggie out of Houston.

I remind myself that if I ever have occasion to engage in conversation with that little cheerleader again I will do so with graciousness and decorum because it very well might land me a massive commission down the road.

Damnit. I don't want to have to call Reggie tonight with the bad news that Bickelworth doesn't want to keep him bad enough to open up the coffers and cough up the cash Reggie deserves. I press the button to turn on the hands-free, and give the voice command to call my assistant.

"Get Bickelworth on the phone," I tell her. She's groggy. It's almost midnight here, which means it's two in the morning in New York.

"Now?"

"Sorry to wake you, Tara. But this is a major deal."

"No problem. I'll ring you back once I've got him on the line."

I hang up, and crank the volume on the stereo. I'm listening to Miles Davis' "Kind of Blue," a jazz classic that almost always calms me down when I get in these moods. John Coltrane improvises liquid sheets of music across the top of the lush ballad, "Blue in Green." I take a deep breath. I'm not calling Reggie with bad news. I'll think of something.

The handsfree rings. I press the button on the steering wheel to answer.

"Zora here," I snap.

"Jackson, it's Bill."

"Tara get you?" I ask.

"Tara? No. I just called you right now."

"On your own."

He sighs. "On my own. Hold on, it's the goddamned call-waiting."

"It's probably Tara. Ignore it."

"Okay. I did some thinking on the drive home."

"You drove yourself? After all those beers? Not wise, my friend."

"I only had one."

"That's what Dick Cheney said after he shot his friend. And me and you, we're not even friends."

Bill laughs. That's good news. He's softening up. "Yeah, well, fun as I think it'd be, I don't have immediate plans to shoot your ass."

"I'll consider myself lucky, then. You ready to deal, Billy?" I ask him. Now my call-waiting is beeping. Tara.

"I'm ready to give Reggie the goddamn extension," Bill tells me with a sigh.

"On the terms we discussed?" I ask.

"Yes."

I won.

We agree to get paperwork going in the morning, and I end the call, triumphant.

My mood lifts instantly. I knew I hadn't lost my touch. The song changes to the sexy mid-tempo "All Blues". I push the pedal to the metal, elated, and drive harder, the flash of city lights outside my window something like the magical lights of a million fairy fireflies, wings beating in time to the intoxicating trill of piano keys whose octaves only go up and up and up.

Mackenzie

Okay, so this is supposed to be the part where I feel like I'm flying through the air, soaring with the comfort and knowledge that I've found the man I am going to spend the rest of my life with. But all I can hear is the totally annoying sound of my own voice in my head, going, what in the heck did you do now, psycho?

I sit in the cab of Dino's truck in my parents' driveway, the new, gigantic diamond engagement ring on my finger. It feels sharp, like it will ruin every sweater I own. I love my sweaters. I wonder in this moment if maybe I don't love my sweaters more than I love Dino. I wonder after that if I love Dino at all. I don't know. Is love being attracted to someone physically, and being happy to see them, but feeling just as happy when they go back to Austin because it means you can breathe again? Is that what love feels like? I think that's what love feels like for my parents, even though I'm not sure about the physical attraction part. I don't want a love like that. I always imagined there would be this other kind of love out there, a love that you felt sad to see go, or at the very least a love that you did not feel relieved was gone; a love that once it was gone you thought about, and it made the idea of the next time you would see them something amazingly totally wonderful to look forward to. I don't really look forward to seeing Dino. I mean, I know he's going to come, and we're going to have dinner and a movie, and that he's going to talk about Dino, and football, and his favorite subject – Dino playing football. But it just doesn't make me want to run out the door when he comes. I walk. I don't hide, right? I mean, I like the guy. I respect him. I admire his skills. I think he's incredibly handsome, and there's nothing better than walking arm in arm with him and seeing the way all the other women look at me like they wish it were them. But it doesn't have that extra something that I always thought real love was supposed to have, but then again the whole idea of real love might just be totally made up by Hollywood.

"Yo! Anybody home?" Dino waves his hand in front of my face and I realize I've zoned out for a minute.

"Sorry. I'm just tired."

It is late. Dark. I see a light on in the house and suspect my mother is waiting up for me in there. I'm exhausted. And maybe a little tipsy from the wine with dinner. All I really want to do is crawl into bed and sleep, and maybe wake up and know that this was all a dream, and not necessarily a good dream.

"So, you think Florida's defense will give me any problems in the BCS title game?"

My eyes are closing on their own. "Dino, sweetie, I'm sorry. As much as I'd like to sit here listening to you talk football, I really have to get inside and go to sleep. I have an early day tomorrow."

"Oh, okay."

He leans in for a kiss. I don't want an open-mouther right now. I really don't. Right now I want a little peck, and a hug maybe, and to go. I want that moment of relief when he drives away. When I go into my room all by myself and close the door and read what I want to read or listen to my headphones without anyone bothering me, when I look at photographs and try to figure out how to do it better next time. But Dino has other plans. There's the tongue. A little thick in the saliva department. Not what I need right now. I pull back.

"Hey," he says, pulling me in again with a big rough hand planted firmly on the back of my neck. "What's the matter?"

"Nothing. I'm just tired. Really tired."

Dino laughs like I've told a joke. "Oh, I get it. We're engaged now, so you have to start practicing the whole frigid wifey thing, 'oh, not tonight dear, I have a headache.' That it?"

"No, that's not it. I'm just tired. I have a six a.m. aerobics class to teach, and a full day after that. The girls have practice and I have to figure out where we're going to do it with the gym a mess, and then I've got to work on my dance routine for the pageant. Plus I have two pounds to lose and you know it's harder to lose when you're sleep deprived. Your body just hangs onto those pounds like you're starving."

"Just one kiss, that's all I ask."

I pull away again, open my car door. "Dino, I love you. I totally do. Have a good night. Get some sleep. You have a long drive in the morning and I need you to be alert, okay?"

Dino gives up and rests his head on the steering wheel in defeat. "Women," he says, shaking his head a little.

"I had a good time tonight," I say, even though I'm not really sure I believe the words.

"I'm going to make you a happy woman," he calls out as I step out of the truck. "You'll see."

"You already have," I say, and he smiles.

Then I shut the door.

Inside the house, I find my mother reading the Neiman Marcus "book" in the living room. This makes me think of Zora Jackson, and that makes me happy. I want to see her again, talk to her, go shopping with her. I can remember the shape of her perfume in my nose, and I want to smell it again, know what it is. Mom looks up at me and I think she looks weird in this room. Totally out of place. She almost never sits in here. No one does. I wonder, really, why we even have a living room. It's one of those things, like marriage. I mean, do you really need the piece of paper if you have all the right feelings? Formality.

"So?" she asks, peeking at my hand. I stuff it behind my back. "Did you have a good night?"

I hold up my hand, and my mother's eyes fill with tears when she sees the ring. She lets the catalog fall to the floor, jumps up and races over to hug me.

"Congratulations," she says.

"Thanks."

"Come, sit down." She leads me back to the sofa, walking with little baby steps like some kind of psycho geisha. After I sit she holds my hand up and looks at the ring again. "He's a good man," she says.

"You said that earlier."

"You'll be very happy."

At that moment, my father enters the room in his pajamas, wearing his reading glasses on a chain around his neck. "I heard girlish squealing in here. Had to come see what all the commotion was about."

My mother and father look at me. "Dino asked me to marry him," I tell my father, even though I know he already knows this.

"And?" He sits in an armchair. Unlike my mother, he doesn't smile or get giddy. Actually, he looks sort of sad.

"And I said yes."

"Isn't it wonderful?" my mother cries.

"It's a big decision. You know that." Are his eyes watering up? They are! No way. He fights it, fights it, and seems to pull the tears back just before one of them might do something embarrassing like slip out of his eye.

"I'm sure she's aware that this is a big decision," replies my mother.

My father's face softens a bit and he shrugs. He doesn't exactly smile. It's like he wants me to think he's smiling but it comes off more like a snarl. "Well, I just want to make sure this is the only time we have to pay for a wedding."

"Don't worry," I say.

"We have to start the plans tomorrow," says my mother. "I can't wait. It's going to be so much fun, the flowers, the menus, the location. Have you thought about that at all, Mackenzie? Where you'd like to have the reception? I mean, naturally the wedding will be at church. But the reception. I'm thinking River Oaks Country Club."

I shrug.

"Well," says mom. "Okay. So we'll have to think about that one."

We? The church? River Oaks Country Club? She's got it all worked out. "Can we talk about it tomorrow?" I ask. "I'm a little tired." Tomorrow. Maybe by then I'll have the balls to stop this whole train before it goes crashing off the cliff.

My mother hops up again. "In a minute," she says. "First, I think we should all have a little something cold to celebrate."

She whirls out of the room humming "so exciting," leaving me alone with my father. He sits forward and studies my face again. Then, in a low tone of voice he says, "You don't have to do it, you know that."

"I know." Why is he doing this to me? Because he totally wants to find a new excuse to fight with mom? This is unfair.

"Your mother wants this more than you do, I think."

"I don't know."

"Of course you do. I know what love looks like, Mackenzie, and I don't see it in your eyes for Dino."

"He's a great catch," I say.

"You're not fishing, you're talking marriage. Lifelong commitment."

"I know."

Dad sighs and rubs the bridge of his nose with his fingertips.

"You okay?" I ask him.

He sighs. "I lost another patient today."

"Oh, gosh. I'm sorry, dad."

He nods.

We sit in silence for a moment. Then he says, "Life is short, Mac. Too damn short."

My mother waltzes back in with three champagne flutes and a bottle of cold Dom Perignon. She hands us our glasses, pours our drinks.

"To the future Mrs. Mackenzie Solis," my mother says with a giddy, almost manic smile. Dad and I raise our flutes, and toast. I take a few sips. Mom asks, "Why the long faces, you two? This is a wonderful occasion."

"I know, mom. It's also really late and I'm pretty tired, so if you guys don't mind I think I'll go to bed now."

"Of course," says my mother. "You get some rest. Tomorrow we'll start thinking about places for the reception. And the dress. Oh my goodness. Amsale. Or Kenneth Poole. You would look so beautiful in a Kenneth Poole. Wouldn't she, honey?"

My father looks at me. "Our daughter would look beautiful in a burlap sack," he says. "She's a beautiful person."

"Sure," I say. I get up. I've never heard my father say anything like this to my mother. My father seems hardly able to make eye contact with me. "Good night you guys."

"We're so proud of you," my mother answers.

Zora

I can't wait to call Reggie to tell him Bill Bickelworth agreed to everything he wanted. I can't wait to tell him, so I dial his home as I walk from the garage to the door to the kitchen.

"You're the best, baby," Reggie tells me. He doesn't sound sleepy, and tells me he's been waiting up to hear from me, watching "Austin Powers" with his wife, Regina. She takes the phone and tearfully thanks me, too. She never wanted to leave Houston, a town where she and their children have laid down roots.

"All in a day's work, my dear," I tell her.

I open the door, enter the kitchen. The lights are off, but there's a faint glow from the lights in the living area around the corner. I hear subtle music playing softly, trumpet. Miles Davis? My daughter was listening to Miles, too? I wonder what she's doing up so late. Then again, it's Saturday night, and she's not a baby anymore.

I round the corner, a smile the size of Texas on my face. But as soon as I see who's sitting on the purple sofa, alone, bobbing his head in time to the music and flipping through a copy of the ESPN Magazine with the long-ass profile of me in it, the smile fades.

"What are you doing here?" I demand.

Yardbird looks up as if he is surprised to see me, even though he had to have heard the garage door and kitchen door opening and closing.

"Zora! Hi."

His shoes are off, lined up neatly by the front door, and socks on his feet look very clean and soft. He's a good-looking kid, as I've already mentioned, but the best thing about him are his eyes, which cast an intelligent, humor-filled vibe. In spite of myself, I feel a warmth spread through my belly at the sight of him.

"What are you doing here, Yardbird?" I repeat. I pull the edges of the green jacket closer together, almost as if to hide how attracted I am to this young man. Sketches of Spain. That's what this album is. One of my all-time favorites. "And where's my daughter?"

"She's in the bathroom," he tells me. "And I'm here because we were studying for a chemistry test next week."

"Chemistry," I say, as if he intended the double-meaning. "Yeah, okay."

He sets down the magazine and looks me plainly in the eye. "There's nothing between me and Lissette."

I smirk to let him know I wasn't born yesterday. "Which explains why you were here earlier today, and now you're back, in the middle of the night."

"No," he says calmly. "Our study group was the reason I was here earlier today, and the reason I'm here now just got home."

I blink at him, not understanding. He sits up straighter, unruffled, self-assured. "I'm sorry?" I say. "What is that supposed to mean?"

"It means I can't stop thinking about you."

I laugh. "Me?"

He looks at me unflinchingly. "Sexy, beautiful, successful, confident." He pauses while the music continues in the background. "With an incredible record collection, and style."

My voice drops to a loud whisper. "I'm old enough to be your mother."

"You would have had to have had me at twelve," he says. "That's young, even for you."

Twelve? That would make Yardbird twenty-four? Five years older than Lissette. Much closer to her in age than he is to me.

"I'm a late-bloomer," he says. "I took some time off after college to play in a band. Toured Europe, the Middle East, Japan."

"A band."

"Guy named Gary Burton." He points to my record collection. "You've got a few of his older records."

My jaw drops without me meaning for it to. "You toured with Gary Burton?"

He smiles at me because he knows I underestimated him and have only now realized it, shrugs. "Ain't no thing, girl, calm yourself," he says. He takes an empty glass off the coaster on the table, stands up and walks across the room, graceful as a dancer, toward the kitchen, stopping just in front of me. "You," he repeats softly. "Are amazing."

"No, I'm not. I'm really not."

He tilts his head a little, fierce. "Had a baby with Ivan Barbosa as a teenager, but went on to study business and law on your own, in a public high school by day and at CUNY at night, a genius. Then Columbia heard about you, and off you went, on scholarship. That's what the New York Times called you. A genius."

"It's not as impressive as it sounds."

"And then, at eighteen, you have the balls to insist on representing your high school sweetheart as his agent, even though there are experienced agents lining up to do it."

"Something like that."

"Ivan lets you do it, and you're the laughing stock of the sports world, a poor, African American teen mamma, thinking she can do some shit like that."

I stare at him and remain mute. Boy's done his homework.

"And then, to everyone's surprise, you know exactly what you're doing. And you get him an incredible deal with the Red Sox, after they draft him. All those 'wherefores' and "unless and untils,' all that legal jargon. The vocabulary don't intimidate you one little iota. You got it like that."

"I'm positively fatigued," I say. "And I'd like to go to bed."

"Okay. I'll leave you alone. But I just want to say, I've never heard anything as amazing as your story, Zora. You get a dream deal for Ivan, and every sports writer sexist asshole in the country has egg on their face for underestimating you. And a career, as they say, is born."

"Something like that."

"You go to Barnard on a full scholarship, then on to Columbia for an MBA, all while starting one of the most successful independent sports agencies in the world without a dime of help from any damn body."

"It's been a long day," I say, measuring my words carefully to not reveal the way my heart dips and sings for this young – very young – man's eyes.

"And you put up with a cheating husband and gracefully send him packing and continue on like nothing's wrong, and from what I can tell you spend the next decade being far, far too generous with that lowlife man."

I look at him and try not to flinch. He's been right about everything but this. I am not going to correct him, however. Instead, I just say, "You should leave now."

"An amazing woman." He holds the glass up. "I'll just wash this, and be on my way."

Lissette comes down the stairs, wearing a gray yoga suit that doubles as pajamas.

"Hi, mom," she says. From the awkward look on her face, I comprehend that Mister Yardbird has told her about his feelings for me. "How was your meeting?"

"Went well," I tell her. "Now, if you and your friend will excuse me, I'm heading up to bed. I've had a very long, very exhausting day."

"Good night, Zora," says Yardbird. "Hope to see you again soon."

"Don't count on it," I say, but I don't mean it at all. I really, truly do hope to see him again.

"I'm counting on it like a metronome," he says. "Slow, steady, reliable. That kind of thing isn't acquired. That kind of thing is born. You are born with reliability and honesty. A man is born with these qualities, Zora. Young or old, it don't matter. He either has them, or he doesn't. And I want you to know that I do; always have, always will."

Lissette lifts a brow at me. My cheeks burn with longing, and humiliation, as I turn away from them, and march up the stairs, hoping to God this old wonderwoman's ass looks as good as young Mister Yardbird seems to think it does.

Mackenzie

I wake up in the hyper blare of my alarm clock at 5 a.m., still dazed from a highly inappropriate, terrifying and ugly sex dream involving Bill Bickelworth. Ugh. What is wrong with me?

I yawn, stretch. It's a good feeling, waking up as simply me, ready to start another day before the sun comes up. Then, almost as soon as I sit up and swing my feet over the edge of the bed, the big, stupid engagement ring snags on the blanket and rips a bit of fuzz out. Then I remember. Crud. I did, in fact, agree to marry Dino. Last night. At PF Chang's. Even though I felt like I was lying when I did it. My parents know. And if my mother lives up to her past reputation as a leading Houston socialite, soon – maybe even by the end of the day – everyone in town will know.

I get up, try to erase the weird dream from memory, fumble through my dresser for another workout outfit, this one pretty basic – a pair of black shorts and a matching black bra-tank. Because it's still early and will likely be cold, I throw on a sweatshirt. Then I pack two more changes of clothes – a warmup suit for work at the high school, and street clothes. I am aware as I choose my outfit - jeans and a dressy shirt with a velvet blazer – that I have picked this particular outfit because it reminds me of something Zora Jackson might wear. And so what? She looks good, and I'd like to look good the way she does.

I slip down the hall to the kitchen, careful to be quiet. I don't want to wake my parents. I don't want to wake them because it's the right, polite thing to do, but I also don't really feel like dealing with them right now. All I want to deal with is the automatic coffee maker, which is on a timer. The scent of freshly brewed coffee fills the house.

As it turns out, I have to deal with my mother anyway. She has left me a cheerful note on the counter, congratulating me yet again and telling me how proud she is of the "wonderful young lady" I've grown up to be. "You are about to start a life that is beyond most people's dreams," she wrote. "Bask in the glory." For all their differences, my mother and Rosie have the note-writing thing in common.

I pour a travel mug of black coffee for myself, grab a banana and my duffle bag, and walk out the front door, locking it behind me.

The drive to the gym is peaceful, with hardly anyone on the road. This is my favorite time of day, the solitary time, and my thoughts move fast. The day is not yet too hot. The air is thick with moisture. A new day coming. It's going to be okay, I tell myself. Dino himself said that he would be able to accept me the way I am, no matter what, that the love he has for me will allow him to get past any secrets I might have. He's a good man. I know this. He even said he doesn't want me to give up my life, so the chances that my marriage will end up looking like that of my parents are slim. My marriage will be different. Very different.

The parking lot to the gym is packed with cars. I gather my iPod from the floor of the car (don't ask me how it ended up there, because the short answer is basically that everything ends up there) and I enter the gym in a slightly groggy state. This is one of those mornings that sleep doesn't want to leave me, coffee or no coffee. The front desk guy says good morning, and buzzes me through the gate. I go straight to the bathroom and lock myself in a stall. I feel like I'm going to have a seizure or something. I am dizzy and a little nauseated. I think it's the coffee and banana on an empty stomach, and maybe a little bit of a hangover from last night. I could use some bread in my stomach. Then there's the whole "I'm not sure I want to get married but it appears I'm getting married anyway" thing.

I exit the stall, go to the sink and splash my face with cold water. I look at my reflection. Am I doing the right thing? A few of my regulars enter the locker room and say good morning to me. I smile and try not to show any of what I'm feeling.

In the aerobics room my usual loyal crowd of housewives and office workers has begun to assemble.

Ashley is here, with her equipment set up in the back row. She doesn't like to draw too much attention to herself here. She's very supportive to show up at my classes like this. I go to her and we embrace. She instantly notices the ring.

"No you didn't!" She holds up my hand and squeals. "Oh my God! How exciting!"

She moves my hand this way and that, examining the goods like a jeweler. I'm realizing people are going to do this a lot, hold up my hand as if it were a display of some kind and not actually attached to my body.

"Mackenzie! It's incredible!"

I smile. It is a gorgeous ring. No doubt. "Am I crazy?" I ask her.

"What? No!" she says. "You are lucky! I'd love to have someone like Dino ask me to marry him!"

"Yeah."

Ashely pulls me in for another hug. "Hey. It's totally normal to get cold feet about something like this," she says. "You are totally doing the right thing, though. Think about it. Rich, handsome, athletic, nice. Rich. Really rich. He's the perfect guy."

I smile at her, glance at the wall clock. Five minutes to go until class begins. I still have to go over my notes for the routine, and get the music ready. "We'll talk about this later," I tell Ashley.

"I want you to tell me the whole thing. How he asked you, all that. Did he get down on one knee?"

"Not exactly."

"Okay, well you'll tell me all about it later on."

"Yeah." I turn and walk to the front of the room, and hop up on to the small stage. I use my personal key to open the black stereo cabinet, and take out the microphone. I clip it onto my belt and then place the headset on. The foam of the mouthpiece smells terrible. I keep forgetting to bring my own. I don't know who uses this thing on before me, but it's pretty disgusting. I take a tissue from the box on the stereo cabinet and try to clean the black foam covering the mouthpiece. It doesn't really help.

By now, because they are gossips, the whole class knows I am engaged. One of the women in the front row – a total type A anorexic fifty-something with leg warmers – asks me who the lucky guy is. I tell her, and the whole group gasps. They are impressed. I stand there, with all the nodding faces and smiles aimed at me, and I realize I did, in fact, do the right thing. Dino is a hero, and people admire him. Maybe, I think, maybe if I concentrate on feeling right about marrying him it will just happen. After all, you don't always wake up before sunrise feeling like teaching an exercise class. But once you force yourself to do it, once the music is pumping and your endorphins are flowing, then it starts to feel right, and natural.

Tired, hungover, nauseated, I smile for the class and say, perky as can be, "Good morning, everyone! Welcome to Step. Is there anyone here who's never taken Step before?"

I pause and look around the packed room. No one raises a hand. "Okay, great. Let's get started then. Begin by checking the supports beneath your benches, to make sure they are firmly in place. The last thing you want is to start stepping with your supports out of place."

Look who's talking.

After class, I shower and get dressed for work. Ashley grills me about the engagement as we do our makeup and hair. She seems genuinely happy for me. When for some stupid reason I get caught up in her excitement and accidentally tell her I'd like her to be my maid of honor, she almost falls over from jumping up and down so ecstatically. Her happiness eases my own uncertainty, and by the time I walk to my car I am feeling almost convinced that I made a good choice. It won't kill me to marry Dino. I can still travel the world. I shouldn't base my decision on a fear that my marriage will just end up looking like my mom and dad. It will be a beautiful wedding. And we'll have an amazingly comfortable life. I'd be crazy not to marry Dino Solis.

But then, as I drive and listen to Leann Womack again, I remember all the reasons I don't want to get married. The biggest one being, simply, that I don't want to get married. My mother calls me while I'm on the road to tell me she's going to make some fitting appointments for me at the bridal shops at Saks and Neiman Marcus.

I get to the school just before eight in the morning, and find that nothing has been done about the gaping hole in the gymnasium ceiling, other than to put a "Wet Floor" sign beneath it. The debris has been swept into a pile but not taken away. I take out the camera and take more photos. You never know.

I go into the principal's office and ask her what she plans to do about the ceiling. She acts like she doesn't know what I'm talking about. When I remind her – and really how could she not have heard about this yet? – she tells me she'll look into it but that it might take her a day or two.

"And what about all the activities the kids need the gym for?"

"They'll have to be canceled," she says.

"But my girls have the state championship coming up next week! They need to practice!"

The principal shrugs. "So do the boys and girls basketball teams. Find somewhere else to practice."

Furious, I stop in the cafeteria to ask the manager if I can borrow the space after school for the dance team. She sips from an enormous paper cup of soda from a nearby gas station, acts unnecessarily official and says she has to authorize it with her higher-ups. I don't understand people who take themselves this seriously. Would it kill her to just say, "Sure, no problem"?

I go to the small, dingy group office off the counseling center, to the desk I share with the special education contractors who come in each day. For now, I'm all alone here. I sit and go through my mail. The registration for the state championship has been completed, and there's a letter listing the time the girls will perform. My heart races a bit at the thought of it. I turn on the aging computer and start to write out a letter to the parents of the girls, notifying them about the competition and asking for volunteers to help us get the costumes in order before then. As I type, my cell phone rings in my purse. I don't recognize the number.

"Hello?"

"Hi. I'm trying to reach Mackenzie de la Garza?"

"This is she."

"Hi, Mackenzie. My name is Natalie Cooper. I'm an assistant photo editor at the Houston Chronicle."

I blink hard, as if clearing my vision will help me to comprehend what she has just said.

"Oh," I say. Seems a stupid thing to say, but it's all that comes out.

"I'm calling about your application for the summer internship."

"Excuse me?"

"I have your application right here. With your portfolio with the cheerleader series. It's quite wonderful, actually."

"What?" I am confused.

"I'm sorry, is this Mackenzie de la Garza?"

Rosie. It had to have been Rosie.

"Yes, this is Mackenzie, but..."

"Cool. Well, to make a long story short, we think your work is interesting."

"You do?" Interesting? Isn't that what people say when they don't want to say something mean?

"Indeed. We're hoping to bring you in for a face-to-face interview sometime in the next week or two, and I wanted to check to see what works for you."

"Is this a joke?" I ask.

She sounds offended. "Why would you think this was a joke?" I feel bad.

"I don't know. Sorry. Just so excited, is all"

"Right. Well, anyway, which day and time works best for you?"

"I'm flexible. Whenever. I'll be there."

She names a date and time, and I distractedly write it down. I have a weird feeling that I have other plans that day, but I can't remember what they are. I'm too busy trying to figure out why my Aunt Rosie would do this to me.

"So, we'll see you then," says Natalie Cooper.

"Yeah. See you then."

"Oh, could you also bring some more examples of your most recent work? We love the cheerleader series, but I think a couple of the people here were wondering if you had more of a hard-hitting news nose."

"News nose?"

"An instinct for harder news."

"Sure, okay."

"Whatever you've got, we'll be happy to look at it."

"No problem."

We say goodbye. Afterward, I call Rosie. She answers her phone sounding very winded.

"Did you send my stuff to the Houston Chronicle?" I demand.

"You bet I did."

"Rosie! How could you do that to me?"

"How could I not? You were never going to do it on your own, and sometimes you just have to give someone a kick-start."

"I'm not good enough, Rosie! And now they want to talk to me in person."

Rosie laughs.

"It's not funny."

"They wouldn't want to talk to you if they didn't think you were good enough, silly."

"Maybe they want to tell me to stop taking photos."

"You think they'd waste their time like that?"

"I don't know."

"You're right. You don't know. You don't know how good you are, and I'm getting sick and tired of it. Just go and see what they have to say. You should be proud of yourself."

We say our goodbyes, and I end the call.

Then, without really knowing why, I punch Zora Jackson's cell phone number into the keypad, followed by "send". I have an urge to talk to her, to ask her how she would handle a situation like this. She's the only woman I can think of in my life other than Rosie who seems totally and completely okay without a man, the only one who might understand the way I feel right now. Maybe there are normal, healthy women who don't need to be married, you know?

She answers after one ring.

"This is Zora," she says. Short, fast, simple, powerful. I would never answer the phone this way.

"Uhm, hi, Zora. This is, uhm, this is going to seem totally strange and weird, but I'm not crazy, I promise."

"Who is this?"

"It's Mackenzie de la Garza. I'm the Ranchers' cheerleader who had your papers."

"Oh." She sounds surprised that I'd call her.

"Uhm. I called because…I guess I called because I really want to talk to you about something personal. It's weird. I mean, how do I say this without sounding like a total and complete freak? I'll just say it. I think we should be friends."

I feel myself blushing, and know that I must sound like a moron to her. She says nothing, and for a moment I worry I've lost the call.

"Hello?" I ask. "You still there?"

"I'm here." She sounds peeved.

"Sorry," I say, completely humiliated. "I mean, I have a really strong feeling about it, and I don't know. Not really friends. I guess. More like mentors. I mean you. Not me. I mean, I think I'd like to just listen to you and your story of your success. I've never met anyone like you and I totally admire everything you've done and you're still so beautiful and smart, and I know this sounds weird but I really want to get to know you better."

My cheeks burn with the flood of warm blood. I am embarrassed. Very. But excited, and more alive than I've felt in a long time.

"Oooo...kay…" She says this as if I were a little strange, which I guess I am.

"I know this seems weird."

"Got that right."

"But I've never met anyone like you and I think that you might be able to help me with something. Something I have to figure out. I'd rather talk about it in person, if you don't mind. This would be easier face-to-face. I know you're probably really busy and totally understand if you don't want to. But I'm not dangerous or anything."

"Why me?"

"I don't really have anyone in my life that I can talk to about any of this stuff and you seem so different from them, all the people I know, and like you'd be easy to talk to and you'd have solutions to things or something."

"You know," she says. "It's funny you called. Just last night, after I saw you guys coming in off the field, I started to think about how it might be a good idea to unionize professional cheerleading."

"Really?" I'm surprised by the turn in the conversation.

"I wanted to talk to some people about it. So here's what I propose."

"Okay."

"We get together for coffee later this morning. I'm only in town until tomorrow. I'll help you with your problem, and you help me understand the world of cheerleaders a little better."

"That would be great," I say.

"Okay, meet me at Café Soleil in a couple of hours."

"Café what?"

"Soleil. It's a nice little independent coffeehouse."

"Oh, okay," I have no idea where Café Soleil is, but I am not about to let the very cool Zora Jackson know how unhip I am. I'll find it.

"You've never been there," says Zora. "Never mind. Let's make this easy. Just meet me at the Starbucks uptown, right across from the Galleria."

"Oh, okay. I know exactly where that is."

Zora continues, "Basically, I'm wondering if there isn't a shitload more money to be made in professional cheerleadering."

"Oh."

Not really, I think. There are way too many girls willing to do it for nothing. I can only imagine what would happen if we started demanding more money. They'd fire us and find other girls willing to do it for free.

"We'll talk."

Then, my heart pounding with more excitement than I felt when Dino asked me to marry him, I wonder just how I might be able to tell a complete stranger all the things I'm too afraid to tell anyone I actually know.

Zora

I sit at the dining table, reading the sports section of the Houston Chronicle, relaxed in my black silk Victoria's Secret pajamas and matching robe. Lissette whistles as she prepares strong, aromatic coffee and a toasted, bagel with lox and cream cheese on it. Not the healthiest breakfast in the world, to be sure, but it's my favorite breakfast in the world, the same one I've been having for as long as I can remember. You can take the girl out of New York, but – well. I like my bagels in the morning. Sue me. The early morning sunlight slants through the trees across the street and filters softly through the many windows of the townhouse, filling it with a gentle, amber glow.

"Who was that?" asks Lissette, pointing at my cell phone.

"I think I might have just been propositioned by a Ranchers cheerleader I met yesterday."

Lissette gives me a look, like she thinks I've lost it, and says, laughing, "She propositioned you?"

"I think so. I mean, if a woman tells you she's been thinking about you a lot and she really wants to see you, that she has never felt such a strong connection with someone, that she admires you and thinks you are amazing, is that a come-on?"

"No."

"But it kind of sounded like a come-on."

Lissette rolls her eyes. "Mom, this is Texas. People are just nice here. It's not New York." She shakes her head like she's so much smarter than her mom. "You're paranoid."

"Yeah. Maybe. Where I'm from we call it street smart."

"So are you going to see her?"

"Yeah. Later today. I'm thinking I might try to be the first woman to unionize professional cheerleaders."

My daughter looks at me like I'm crazy.

"Seriously. They get nothing. But they're worth a lot of money to the teams. If you think about it, it's a feminist issue actually."

"That's why they wear skimpy outfits. Because they're such big feminists."

"It's a money issue."

"Mom?"

"Daughter?"

"No. It's never gonna happen."

"You ready for your chemistry exam?" I ask, changing the subject.

Lissette screws up her face as if I've insulted her. "Of course."

"That's my girl," I say, remembering how, when Lissette was barely in the first grade at The Spence School, her teacher told me she had an unusual gift for math and science. It was a prophecy of sorts. Lissette went on to win several science fairs in middle and high school, and upon graduation had scholarship offers from several top engineering schools. She chose Rice because she, like I, loves Houston. Unlike most prep school kids who migrate East for college, Lissette was ready to escape the misery of cold and the snow, and so far, she says, Houston fits her as well as the Seven jeans she's so fond of. She's already dressed for school, makeup done, hair blown straight. Lissette is studying chemical engineering, of all things, with her sights set on literally becoming a rocket scientist.

She brings a thick white mug of the coffee and sets it in front of me. I lift the warm cup in my hands, enjoying the heft of it. Though my tastes run to the modern and minimalist, I prefer my coffee in substantial pottery. I take a sip, eyes closed, savoring the aroma and creamy texture.

"Perfect," I tell her.

"Chemists make good cooks," she says with a grin. She lifts her keys from the computer table at the end of the kitchen closest to the garage door.

"You takin' off?" I ask her.

She nods as she pops a piece of bagel in her mouth. She pours coffee into a pink shiny travel mug. "You going back to New York today?"

I consider this question. I was originally scheduled to go back today. But the ballet is tonight. The ballet I shouldn't attend with my lecherous ex-husband, but which I'm afraid I'm going to attend anyway.

"I think I'll extend the trip a couple of days, spend some time with you."

Lissette smiles at me. "And the cheerleader."

"Ha-ha, very funny."

"And daddy."

"Maybe."

Lissette's smile grows. "If I don't see you before you leave, have a good time with him tonight. I won't wait up for you. I know he's hurt you, mom, but I think he's really finally changed."

I wonder if my daughter knows about the incident with Ivan and the nanny. I assume she does, because it has been mentioned a bit in the media, but we've never talked about it. She is probably just pretending not to care - or choosing, because this man is her father, not to believe it.

"Is that what he told you?" I ask.

"Yeah."

Nice to know the man is lying to our child, too.

"What time will you be home?" I ask her, out of habit and also as a diversion from the uncomfortable topic of me going out with her father.

She observes me carefully, leans into one hip, crosses her arms over her chest. Girl looks like she thinks she's grown.

"Mom, I don't want to upset you, but I don't think you should keep asking me what time I'm going to be home and stuff like that. I'm not a little kid."

I feel my face flush with embarrassment. "Of course. I know."

"Quit worrying."

She sounds so much like me when I was a teenager I almost laugh out loud. "Go. Don't be late. For class, I mean. Come home whenever you like, miss adult person."

"I've never been late for class," she tells me. She might be grown up, but she still cares mightily what I think of her.

Lissette hesitates, sips her coffee, draws a deep breath and says, "You should also know I'm going out tonight too, and I might not come home at all," she tells me in a way that seems to pain her. The pinched way she speaks, almost flinching, with one hand on the door to the garage, ready to bolt, tells me that she's been meaning to tell about him, whoever he is, for a while, and has only now summoned up the courage. I am overcome by the urge to find him, strangle him with my bare hands. But I realize this is unreasonable. Lissette is nineteen years old. Almost twenty. A grownup.

"Condoms," I tell her. "That's all I'm gonna say."

Lissette lifts a hand as if it might shield her from my lecture. "Mom, please. I'm not an idiot."

164

"I never said you were."

She smiles shyly, and I realize she's in love. "His name is Owen."

"Owen."

"Owen Leiberman. He's a chemist, too."

"In school with you?"

"He's a graduate student. You'd really like him. He's really funny and super smart"

"How long have you been seeing him?"

"Three months."

"And you're only now telling me?" Bad mom. I didn't mean to sound so shrill. Honestly.

She sighs. "No offense, mom. But it's like it's just been me and you forever and now that I'm in Houston, I don't know. I like my freedom. I just feel like I don't want to have to tell you every little detail of my life."

"You want space?"

"Kind of."

"Space granted. Get out of here."

Lord, but it's hard to be a cool mom. For so many years I went out of my way not to be a cool mom. I wanted to be a mom Lissette listened to, a mom who set limits and made rules. A fear-inducing mom. The whole transition from overseer to roommate is a little hard to take.

"Love you," she says.

Hard to take, but with its rewards.

"Love you too, Lissette."

Then, my daughter – taller, smarter, and older than I ever imagined she'd be – leaves me. On her way to her own life. A life that has very little to do with me anymore. A life that, apparently, involves something "really funny and super smart," named Owen Leiberman.

I sit in the silence of the empty house and think. I sip at the coffee, but somehow it doesn't taste as good as it did a few minutes ago, before I knew about Owen Leiberman. Owen Leiberman makes life bitter. I don't understand it. There was a time when I looked forward to having more time to myself. Man. I'd say I've spent the better part of the past nineteen years looking forward to Lissette going to college. When Lissette was four or five, needing more attention that I could give her, I agonized over having to hire a nanny to help me with her. I cried myself to sleep some nights, pummeled by the guilt of a busy working single mom, dreaming of the day I wouldn't have to worry about my child so much it was like a permanent case of indigestion. I used to meet mothers whose children were grown and gone, and I envied them for finally being able to be selfish again. Their nails always seemed freshly painted. I remember all those days when I didn't feel like I had time to do a proper job with my hair or makeup, because the little girl Lissette was needed me to play with her, to be fully and completely with her in the few moments we had together before I ran off to school, or to the office, and she went off to preschool with my mom or, later, the nanny. Back then, I dreamed of the day when she would be able to take care of herself and not need me so much that I allowed her needs to supersede mine in almost every way. I used to fantasize about having my life to myself again, going to the gym when I wanted to, taking as long as I wanted at the salon, going to a movie by myself at night.

Well, well, I tell myself, the time for my emancipation has come, faster than I imagined it would. And somehow, stupidly, all I can seem to do is miss my little girl.

Mackenzie

Okay, so I'm totally and completely a nervous wreck. I'm standing in the very long line at the Starbucks uptown where Zora asked me to meet her. It's one of the bigger Starbucks I have ever seen, with very high ceilings, the whole space sort of designed around the circular center of the room. I am suddenly a little self-conscious about the jacket and the tank top, wondering if I am too obviously dressed like Zora. I did not think I was going to actually see her today, or I wouldn't have dressed exactly like she did yesterday. I didn't expect to see her today and now I'm going to. How sucky is that? I wring my hands and try to look cool. No sign of Zora. Then I'm at the front of the line.

"What can I get for you, miss?" asks the barista.

"Just give me a nonfat latte," I say, knowing that I should have probably ordered a straight mint tea or something else with zero calories. But it won't kill me to have just a tiny bit of nonfat milk.

As the barista prepares my drink, I look over my shoulder at the door just in time to see Zora come in. She scans the room and spots me quickly. She wears dark trouser jeans and a crisp white tailored button-down shirt in some kind of satiny cotton, low-cut. She has a necklace made of large dark-glass beads around her neck, and strappy sandals. As she walks toward me with that confident grace of hers, I notice her toenails and fingernail are perfectly painted French. She wears her hair up today, with just a couple of loose curls falling around her face. She removes her dark glasses as she nears me, and her eyes smile, friendly but not overly so.

"Hi," I say.

"Mackenzie." She looks me up and down with a wry grin. "That outfit looks familiar."

Oh gosh. No. Did she really just say that. "It does?" I play dumb. Sometimes that's the best policy.

At the bar the worker shouts, "Mackenzie, nonfat latte for Mackenzie!"

I grab my drink and Zora tells me she's going to the back of the line and will meet me at a table. She doesn't ask. She tells. I like that. I want to be like that. How the hell can I learn to be like that?

I find a table near a window, without too many crumbs on it, and sit. I watch Zora. She is busy checking her mobile phone and doesn't notice me staring at her. My heart begins to pound with nervousness. What am I doing here? I mean, what am I going to tell this woman?

Finally, Zora joins me. She's got a cold green shake of some kind, with mountains of whipped cream on top.

"Raspberry green tea, Frapuccino," she says.

"Yummy."

She sips her drink and sizes me up critically. I mentally kick myself for saying "yummy," because Zora Jackson probably outgrew that word twenty years ago. Zora looks at her phone again, and turns it to vibrate.

"So, Mackenzie, before we get to the reason that I'm here, let me be totally direct with you and I hope you'll return the favor."

"Okay."

"I have never in my life had another woman tell me the things you told me on the phone today."

I gulp and try to look normal.

"And in the interest of direct communication, I just want to ask you something that's been bugging me."

"Okay."

"Is this how you usually make friends, or is there some other reason for all this?"

I take a deep breath and tell myself that no matter what I say there's nothing to lose. She can't hurt me or anything like that.

"Okay," I say. "It's like this. I don't know how to say this, but I'm going to do my best."

"I think you should just say exactly what you're thinking. There's nothing I hate more than indirect communication. I think you deserve to know that about me."

I look around the café and try to keep the blushing to a minimum. Then I force myself to look directly at Zora.

"This is not how I usually make friends. This is nothing like anything I've ever done before. And gosh. This is sort of weird and embarrassing, but the thing is, I just got engaged to Dino but there are all these things I wanted to do in my life first, and I don't think I'm really totally ready to get married until I have some questions about myself answered for myself." I stare at her and try to see if she understands what I'm getting at.

"Keep going," she says, her brow creasing with growing worry.

"Uhm. Okay. Well, has anyone ever told you that you look like Nia Long? You know, the actress?"

Zora furrows her brow. "Mackenzie? This isn't very direct communication we're having here."

"Sorry. It's just not that easy."

"Do you want me to help you?"

I nod, weakly.

"Okay," she says. "I have some theories about you, and this. So I'll throw them out there and you can nod yes or no. That's all you have to do."

My heart zips along, and I feel like I can hardly breathe. I can't believe I'm doing this.

"Theory number one: You are being friendly toward me in the hopes of helping Dino get a good agent who will in turn get him a good deal and thereby secure your finances for the rest of your life."

"No."

"Good, because that would have been an NCAA violation. Theory number two. You're a lonely woman who doesn't have very good social skills."

"No."

"Okay. That just leaves number three. And I have to tell you, I am very, very straight."

"Me too," I say. She laughs at this. "No, seriously, I am."

Zora stares at me for a long moment.

"You want to know what I think?" she asks thoughtfully. "I think you've done something a lot us women do. You've confused sex with admiration and support. It's the basis of cheerleading, actually."

No, I think. I haven't. But I don't say anything because I cannot even believe she's assumed I wanted to be with her like that.

"Right after Ivan and I divorced I got wasted, and slept with this gay female soccer player I represented. It was the only time I've ever slept with a client other than my husband, and I was vulnerable. And pissed. I hated all men because of what he did to me."

I am so uncomfortable now, I can't speak. I just force a smile and hope no one around us is listening in.

"As much as I hated men back then, I realized I am biologically programmed to be attracted only to men. I really admired that woman. She's one of the best in the world, and very fierce. She's gorgeous. But at the end of the day I realized that I'd crossed the admiration wires with the sex wires. We women are taught from the earliest time on that to be someone we have to be with someone who's someone. We sexualize our ambitions. We substitute sex for the real feelings of admiration that might best be served through mentorship, or friendship. Does that make sense, Mackenzie?"

I nod a little. "I think so. But-"

Zora smiles kindly at me. "You would not believe how much I've thought about this whole issue. We are trained to think of other women as sexual from the time we see our first fashion magazine cover or Barbie doll. But the fact of the matter is, when it finally comes right down to it, most women aren't all that interested in being with other women that way."

"But I think maybe you misunderstood-"

"Don't worry," she tells me with a wink. "This is our secret."

"Uhm, but I'm not – I'm not like that. That's not why-"

"Not another word about it," she tells me.

"But-"

"Tell me the real deal. What's really on your mind? What's your real goal? Who do you really want to be?"

"A photographer," I say softly. "That's the reason I wanted to talk to you."

"Yeah?" She beams at me and leans back in her chair, sizing me up. "Good for you. Tell me about that."

I try to forget that she has completely misread me, because what harm would it do in the end, and I tell Zora about the interview with the Chronicle. She looks at me like she's seeing me for the first time.

"I just think I'd rather do that than marry Dino, and everyone I know thinks I would be crazy to do that."

"Can't you get married and do photography?" Zora asks me as though I were a complete idiot.

"No. I mean, I could, I guess. But Dino's so – I don't know how to say this nicely."

"Then don't."

"You're right. I shouldn't say it."

"That's not what I mean," she tells me, seeming to lose patience. "I mean say it the way it needs to be said. Niceness is overrated, MacKenzie."

"Okay." I hesitate, because I haven't had any practice being direct like this, and honest, and possibly cruel. "Dino's a self-centered jerk, and I feel like I would rather spend my energy working on myself than feeding his bottomless pit of an ego."

Zora's eyes dance with pleasure at my words, and she nods approvingly. "Well said."

"People will think I'm crazy. He's worth a bundle. He's famous."

"I don't think you're crazy," she says.

"Really?"

"Really. Listen to me. I've been around professional athletes all my life. With very few exceptions they've all got bottomless pit egos, and their wives are some of the unhappiest people I've ever known. If the men aren't cheating on them – and most of them cheat, I don't care what anyone tells you, it's a simple fact of being a male full of testosterone on the road with groupies everywhere you look – then they're hardly ever home. It's not a partnership. It's no way to live your life. I wouldn't advise it. It sounds terrible, but those are my honest to God feelings on the matter."

"So I don't have to marry him, you don't think?" I ask, as the tears of relief fill my eyes.

"Honey," she tells me with a big old smile, "you don't have to do anything you don't want to do with your life. It's your life, and you only get one."

"Thank you," I tell her, the tears brimming and sliding down my cheeks. "You are such an inspiration. Not a lot of women would have had the guts to leave a man like Ivan Barbosa. But you did it, and look at you now."

It might be my imagination but Zora looks a little uncomfortable at this. She averts her gaze and narrows her eyes at the bright light outside the window for a moment.

"Yeah," she says with an awkward smile and a cynical look at her drink. "Look at me now."

Zora

I remember this feeling so well. Sitting in the passenger seat of Ivan's car, Dominican music on the stereo, breathing in the heady spice of his cologne as we pulled up to the valet at one or another exalted restaurant. I feel posh, opulent, and taken care of, even though I know it's nothing more than an illusion, polished and gleaming as the finest diamond. If that little cheerleader could see me now, she would know exactly what sort of hypocrite I am. Happily for her, she has no idea I'm here. Maybe she'll make the right choices, and fare better in love than I did.

The car is a Lotus Elise that Ivan rented for his weeklong stay in Houston, in a color he laughingly recounts the rental office manager referring to as puce.

"I thought he was saying puke," Ivan tells me. His smile is as fresh and seemingly harmless as always, a seductive smile because it broadcasts boyish fun and humor. "I was like, look, asshole, I pay four-hundred dollars a day for a car, it better not be the color of no puke."

He looks at me with a half-grin, his eyes shiny and beautiful. "You know, it'd be so much easier if everyone in this country just spoke Spanish, eh?"

Ivan slices the severe, sharp sports car up to the valet stand in front of Mark's American Cuisine, an elegant restaurant situated in a captivating building that used to be a church of some kind. The three men with red vests at the stand eye the car with openmouthed admiration, their sense of reason and propriety temporarily suspended by the flow of testosterone to the brain.

"Most romantic restaurant in Houston," says Ivan as the valet scurries over to open my door. It's the third time this evening he's reminded me that he chose "the most romantic restaurant in Houston" for our date.

"Don't get your hopes up," I tell Ivan.

The door opens, but the car is so low I have to use the valet's hand to help me up out of the seat. I feel my age at moments like this. There was a time when I would have thought this car was sexy and cool, but that time has long gone. Now it strikes me as immature for a man nearing forty to be renting a car like this. Who is he trying to impress? Then I remember. Every one of the three wives he's had since me has been younger than the last.

I stand on the curb, the light breeze fluttering the hem of my new dress. I'm not proud of the fact that I scrambled off to my favorite boutiques this afternoon, after meeting MacKenzie, in search of the perfect date dress. I'm not proud that my adrenaline pumped as I tried on more than two dozen dresses, twirling this way and that in the dressing room mirror like a schoolgirl proud of her flounce and fluff. I chose a flowing black long-sleeved dress with a low V neckline, lined, with a flared skirt, designed by

Diane vonFurstenberg. I'm wearing sexy high-heeled black leather boots by Isabel Fiore that cost more than the dress, with a dainty black clutch purse that makes me feel somewhat naked. I guess I'm a little too used to the giant, shoulder-breaking briefcase.

With my free hand, I hold down the edge of my skirt. I've forgotten that awkward sense you get when you're in a dress that the wind might make you a flasher at any moment. Considering the tiny thread of thong that is my underwear at the moment, the view would likely be spectacular if my gracious exit from the car misfired. Usually, I wear pants. Suits, jeans, it doesn't matter. More than once I've had men joke that I'm a woman who "wears the pants," meaning that I'm a threatening butch or something, but the saying never made sense to me. Given a choice of pants or a skirt, I'd almost always choose pants. Who wouldn't? You can't run to catch your plane in a dress without great risks. You can't climb a fence to get a baseball. But here I am, standing in front of, apparently, the most romantic restaurant in Houston. In a dress. Why? That's easy. Because I remember the way Ivan's eyes would dance when I wore dresses, and for some stupid reason I'm going for that reaction in him again. The cynic in me suspects he likes dresses because it means easier pussy access for him. The loser in me is certain there's something seriously wrong with me. But the woman in me is tired of celibacy, and if that means having a one-night-stand with my ex-husband, so be it.

I watch Ivan slip cash into the valet's hand. The valet bows his head like he worships Ivan, a move Ivan seems entirely too comfortable with. Ivan wears black trousers that seem custom-built for his incredible legs and ass, a crisp white button-down shirt, with the top couple of buttons undone to show off his gold chains. His hair is freshly cut, short, and a diamond stud gleams in his right earlobe. He looks like a businessman, if businessmen could be mouthwateringly well-built, tall and sexy.

Damn, he looks good in those pants.

Ivan looks up, smiles those Don Juan teeth at me as if he has read my mind, and reaches me in four athletic strides. Then, as if no time has passed since we were married, he slips his arm comfortably around my waist and guides me inside the restaurant. While the cynic in me watches in disgust, the woman in me allows herself to be excitedly and expertly guided. I never wanted to divorce this man. He ruined things by disrespecting me. I never stopped loving him, and I probably never will.

This is my first visit to Mark's, and as soon as we enter the chic restaurant to be instantly dwarfed by the soaring, dramatically arched church ceiling, I wonder why I haven't come before. This is exactly the kind of restaurant I love. The elegant tangerine walls glow warmly, the dark wood of the floor shines with the mellow, gentle light. The scent of garlic, fresh bread and olive oil swirl through the room, the subtle murmur of genteel conversation underscored by the elegiac refrain of a string quartet. My mouth begins to water. I gulp, admiring how the architects have kept with the themes of the original structure in the renovation. I don't mean to gasp at the sheer scale of the bullet-shaped two-story medieval-style pointed arch windows, but I do. If I hadn't majored in business, I likely would have become an architect. Ivan knows this. Before I found out about his lovers, we took a trip to Europe, focused on medieval churches. He is well aware of my love for classical European church architecture, and I know this has something to do with his choice of venue. Hand to throat, I try to blink back the tears that have caught me by surprise. The beauty of this place reminds me of all the moments I've had to miss out on because Ivan forced me to divorce him.

"Thought so," says Ivan, cocksure. I smirk quickly at him as a reminder to keep his hopes down, and turn back to the restaurant. Ivan, meanwhile, turns his attention to the hostess, who efficiently whisks us off to a quiet corner of the restaurant she refers to as "the cloister," a name I will assume is held over from the structure's days as a house of worship. As Ivan scoots my chair out for me with a confident, sexy smile on his face – and no small amount of carnal intent in his gaze – I realize he has chosen the perfect place for me to worship him. Like all great manipulators, he is attentive to the tastes and values of his victims, convincing as a car salesman. He has chosen a restaurant that I suspect will fit into the bulls-eye of my palate.

An hour later, my stomach filled with the duck prosciutto, grilled Chilean sea bass with crispy plantains and tequila-lime sauce, and raspberry shortbread tart that made up my meal – not to mention a few borrowed bites of Ivan's grilled veal medallions in Marsala-morel sauce – I lean back, completely content. After you've lived in New York, it's hard to find a meal that impresses you anywhere else, except maybe London, Paris or Los Angeles. But this one did the trick. I sip my espresso and allow the delicate dizziness of the wine, the food, the atmosphere, the company, penetrate every pore. Across from me, Ivan stares into my eyes, the sexy, playful grin he's worn most of the night replaced by that intense intelligence, that insightful and slightly tortured look, that made me fall in love with him in the first place.

"What are you thinking?" I ask him. Stupid question. He baits me with these looks. I'm aware of that. And I fall willingly into the trap.

"I'm thinking that we should go back to my hotel," he says simply.

I feel my eyes narrow in disappointment, as if he's slapped me. I was hoping that the expression on his face meant something more than a bedroom romp was on his mind. I was hoping it meant he had some profound insight into what went wrong with us.

"You game?" he asks, employing the athlete's most overuse cliché.

"Sure, I'm game." As in prey. I smile sadly. The waiter brings the bill and Ivan's credit card back to the table for him to sign. As he does, he watches me with growing concern.

"What's wrong?" he asks as the waiter leaves.

"Nothing," I lie. "Everything's great."

"No, something's wrong."

"I just wish it could have been like this from the day we married," I say.

Ivan reaches for my hand, and squeezes it. "I know. I'm sorry. But why don't we try to make it work now, and leave everything else in the past?"

"I don't know."

"We could even get married again, Zora."

I laugh out loud at this one.

He looks at me with the attitude of a mourner. "I'm serious. I've changed. I've been through so much, learned so much. I'm ready to make a real commitment to a woman I love now. I know what love means now."

"We'll talk about it." I don't want to be happy to hear these words. But I am. I don't want to believe them, but I do. It's all I've ever wanted in my personal life, for this man I've loved for so long to wake up and realize he needed to grow up and that growing up would mean loving me forever. It's not logical, of course I realize that. I'm not an idiot. I know how manipulation works, how to do it, who to do it to. I do it for a living. So there is a large part of me wondering if this latest proclamation for Ivan is nothing more than his newest set of lies.

"I'm at the Icon, let's talk it over there," he suggests. "Great tubs there."

Stupidly, I agree. Sometimes, I suppose, being in bad company is actually better than being alone. Isn't it? And sometimes, people actually do change. Don't they?

Mackenzie

I go back to work feeling a little bit dirty for having been completely misunderstood, and a little bit cleansed for having been totally understood at the same time, like I need to wash my face for an hour, and maybe floss for about that long, but also like I've finally figured something out. And that something is pretty basic. I don't want to marry Dino. I don't completely discount the idea that I might one day become a photojournalist.

The cafeteria Nazi has finally gotten the all-important approval from her higher-up" that she's been waiting for, and my girls have gathered in the space that will forever smell of tater tots. I've salvaged the boom box from the gym, and set it up on one of the rickety cafeteria tables. I tell the girls I'm sorry about the space, the floor of which still has not been swept up since lunchtime, and I try to turn it around so that they will see it as a challenge, so that they will work extra hard to make something big happen in Austin next week.

"Just think, if you can excel here you can excel anywhere!"

The girls stare blankly at me and let me know I'm pushing the limits of logic with this one.

I lead the girls in some warm up moves and stretches, and then I cue the music and count them off. At first, they seem shaky. I stop them, talk them into focusing. And then we do it again. And again. I make the girls run this routine until they finally get it right.

And then, and only then, I let them go and head home to change for my own date. With Justin.

An hour later, I meet him on the sidewalk just outside the Houston Center for Photography. He wears dark, nearly black, jeans and a black button down shirt over a T-shirt with the word "Reluctant Gringoso" across the chest. He's got another pair of those trendy sneakers on, and his hair is messy without looking sloppy, as if he measured every bit of chaos in just the right amount. He looks good, and artistic. I, meanwhile, am in a pair of True Religion jeans, with a tunic-style top cinched with a wide belt across my hips, and a pair of pointy-toed black pumps. I wanted to look artistic, too, but not like I was trying too terribly hard. I also still want to dress like Zora, who has risen in my mind to the top of the human beings in the world I most need and want to imitate.

I tell myself as I walk up to him that this is nothing more than an evening looking at photos with a friend. So why have I told my mother I was rehearsing with Ashley at the gym? It's not because of me. It's because of her. She would be suspicious.

"Hey, you!" calls Justin. It doesn't sound nearly as weird as you'd think. It actually sounds sweet. He turns toward me with a smile. "I was starting to think you might not show."

"Why?"

"Just afraid you wouldn't come." He shrugs.

"I'd have called if I wasn't planning to come."

He looks at me with a certain warmth and insecurity in his eyes that I find alarming. Dino never looks all that warm, or insecure for that matter. "You look beautiful," says Justin.

His eyes stray to my left hand.

"Wow. Check out the bling. Football guy?"

"Yeah."

Justin looks hurt and disappointed, but keeps it to himself.

"Shall we?" he says, gesturing to the door.

We enter the photography space, and I am instantly soothed. The white walls, the cool air. And nothing but photographs. I could live here. Justin offers to pay my admission, and I notice his wallet looks a little ragged. That's never a good sign. Dino's wallet is shiny, leather and new, full of crisp bills. Justin's looks like it's been through the washer a few times, and like it might lock with Velcro. I insist on paying my own way. "Not a date, remember?" I say.

He shrugs and stuffs the scruffy wallet into his back pocket again.

We walk into the main gallery, a large rectangular room. The featured photojournalist's work is displayed on every wall, with small descriptions on cards beneath them. We join the crowd in looking at the photos. The first is of a young man's stiff, naked corpse on a slab of concrete, being washed by a man and prepared for burial. The naked body, face down, looks healthy enough, strong, smooth, almost as if he were at a spa, until you get to the head, which has been blown open. I gasp. The image is beyond horrifying, but done in such a beautiful way, photographically, that you can't help but see the humanity of all those involved.

"Wow," says Justin over my shoulder. "That's pretty intense."

I nod, but cannot find words to say. This is what I want to do. This magic. I want to be able to take one image, to find the right time and place to snap the shot, that will communicate more than any words ever could.

Justin speaks again. "I wonder how the photographer feels when he takes a shot like that. If he cries, or if he just gets numb after a while. I can't imagine."

We move on to the next photo. Grief-stricken men use a concrete wall to hold themselves up beneath a shockingly normal, beautiful blue sky. The caption says their village has just been invaded and they've lost family members, civilians. Anyone, I think, could have taken a photo of grieving men. But this photographer made an effort to include the sky, the normal, everyday sky, and the effect is chilling. This could happen to anyone, it seems to say. These are normal people caught suddenly in the most abnormal and horrific of experiences.

"This guy's good," says Justin, referring to the photographer.

"No kidding," I say.

"And I think you're as good as he is."

I purse my lips as if he's told a bad joke. "Very funny."

"I wasn't trying to be funny, Mackenzie. Rosie showed me your stuff. I really do think you're that good."

"Okay, thanks."

I walk away from Justin without looking him in the eye. I don't know if he means what he says, or if he's just trying to flatter me. I want to be as good as this photographer. More than anything in the world. I don't even want to think about it because I feel like I'll start to cry.

The next shot is of a spiral type of notebook, with row after row of blue ink filling the pages, a close-up shot of several hands leafing through it. The caption tells us the list is of the newly dead brought to the cemetery after the invasion of the village. One of the hands, wearing a lovely ring, hangs limp with despair. You don't need to see a face to know what this man feels. It is all right there, in his gesture, in the hand that can't find the strength to lift the page in the book. The hand of a man who has lost a wife, or a child. A hand that does not know where to go from here.

There are more. Honey-tinted sunset shots from the Midwestern plain states, of small-town life that the photographer tells us in captions is disappearing. Boys shooting BB guns, others getting dressed in the ever-familiar football locker room, skinny but trying to seem like men. There are shots from Havana, one of a man, a cigarette barely dangling from his lower lip, carrying a small dog in his bare arms like a baby. At first I think the dog must be dead, or injured, from the intensity of the last series of photographs in Iraq, but this is not the case. The dog and the man are on their way to the boardwalk in Havana to enjoy a cool breeze on a hot day. The juxtaposition of the normal against the horrific is fascinating to me, because there really is not a difference. Life doesn't suddenly look like a scary movie when bombs start to fall on unsuspecting villagers. Life looks like life, and death appears as part of the whole mess. There is no eerie soundtrack, no warning. This is the photographers strength, I think, his ability to make the horrible look commonplace – the statement being that humankind must change.

"What are you thinking about?" asks Justin.

"I want to do this," I say. The words come out small, breathless, weak. But this isn't how I feel. I feel strong when I look at these images, like I could actually do something like this. Photography is a language, I think, and I was born fluent.

"You should," he says. Then he surprises me by taking my left hand in his own and squeezing it. "You totally should."

I know I should take my hand out of Justin's. But I don't. I just let him hold it, ring and all. Our fingers don't move, as if neither of us knows quite what to do with this. I finally look at his eyes. They're serious and funny at the same time, eyes that are smarter than any I've ever looked into. Looking at Justin feels like being naked. Like he can see everything I'm thinking.

"This isn't supposed to be a date," I say softly.

"Rosie thinks you don't really want to marry Dino," he tells me. "That you're with him because your mom likes him so much."

I feel the back of my throat lock, like I'm preparing to throw up or cry. "She said that?"

Justin does not answer. He just looks at me, and moves a little closer. I feel his eyes turn toward my lips. "You really are pretty," he says.

Just then, someone at the front of the room taps a microphone. I drop Justin's hand, and turn to see the photographer himself.

"Come on!" I tell Justin, trying to sound normal. Trying to focus on my real purpose for being here, which is to listen to one of the best photojournalists in the nation discuss how he got to where he is – and figure out how I might be able to do that someday, too.

I find two empty seats in the back row, and when Justin joins me I cross my arms tightly over my chest, my hands hidden somewhere in my armpits.

Zora

As the valet at the Hotel Icon in downtown Houston opens the door to help me out, I remember all those times when I was in this position – in the passenger seat of Ivan's various luxury cars at various hotels – as his wife. Back then, a valet's hand extended to help me up was a thrill, a source of pride. I had made it. Not only, I then thought, had I made it as a businesswoman, but I had found love. The one thing I'd always wanted. But now? Being helped out of Ivan's car by a valet for the second time in one night? Now I feel like a liar. Dirty. I can't explain exactly what the heaviness I feel is, or where it comes from, only that I am almost ashamed to have this man see my face as he helps me out.

"Good evening ma'am," he says. "Welcome back."

Welcome back. He is assuming that I am staying here at the hotel too, because the car has been here, and the driver of the car. Welcome back, indeed.

"Thank you," I say, smoothing the sides of my dress I was so proud of this morning but which feels like a tragic attempt at a normal life with an abnormal lover.

Ivan slips some money into the valet's hand, and joins me. The doorman to the hotel opens the door for us, and welcomes us back again. We enter the hotel, and I instantly love it.

"Nice," I say of the enormously high ceilings and the retro furnishings.

"This used to be a bank," says Ivan. "Couple years ago they redid the whole thing."

"It's beautiful."

"Ain't got nothin' on you," says Ivan.

I look around at the antique tables, classic oil paintings, and retro-style telephones, at the Asian lamps and busy, colorful Persian carpets, the dripping chandeliers.

"Hold on a second," I say to Ivan. I backtrack to the front desk and ask the girl working there who did the interior design for the hotel. She asks me to hold on, goes to a back room for a moment, and returns.

"A company out of San Francisco called Candra Scott and Anderson."

I commit the name to memory. I might have to call them to redo my New York apartment at some point. I've never seen décor so eclectic and yet perfectly suited to the time period. Wonderful. The balance of whimsical elements with serious pieces is perfect.

"You and your design," he says.

"Hey, you picked this place."

"It's got good design," he says.

"Very funny."

"Actually, this new friend of mine picked it out for me, Yvette."

For a second my blood runs cold at the mention of another woman's name.

He looks at me and laughs. "Don't worry. She's a teammate's girl. She's big on design, like you. Seriously, you don't have to worry anymore, baby. I'm not like that anymore. In fact, when we get married again, I want you to go ahead and hire the company that did this hotel if that's what makes you happy. You can redo my houses. Any way you want."

Happy. I think that the only chance this man ever had to make me truly happy was truly blown by him, years ago. So why am I still here, behaving like an impetuous girlchild? Because I'm a sucker, that's why. Because part of me wants so badly to believe this man I consciously twist my brain upside down so that everything he says sounds right and makes sense. We walk past the restaurant and bar, cavernous spaces with red velvet chairs, sumptuous two-story curtains, and perhaps the largest wine glasses I've ever seen. They're almost like fragile bulbous fishbowls. I love this place, and part of me wishes we were only going for drinks instead of going – well, wherever we're going. Nowhere good. I should be more disciplined about this, but I can't help myself with this man. Ivan leads me to the elevator, and presses the up button. I ruminate over the similarities to earlier in the day, and wonder if I wasn't behaving like him toward the poor little cheerleader. With the arrogance of Ivan. He grins at me like he used to, maudlin as hell, and I want so much to hate him, but can't. I melt when he smiles at me, convince myself that my never-ending patience and love for him will finally work as a panacea. Maybe. Maybe it'll work this time. Maybe he's changed. Some men take longer to grow up than others, I tell myself. He's not young anymore. Maybe he's finally come to his damn senses.

"You okay?" he asks, stroking my cheek as we wait.

"I don't want you to hurt me again," I say. I can't believe how pathetic I sound.

The elevator bell dings, and the doors slide open like a challenge, like a question I need to answer. Will I be stupid enough to do this? I feel Ivan's hand on the small of my back and he says, "Sometimes pain is a choice you make." He pushes me into the elevator.

"What do you mean by that?" I ask as he slides his keycard into the slot that allows him to operate the elevator. The doors close with a whump, and he turns to me, pushes his glorious, masculine self against me and buries his head in my neck. I ache for him. I remember the smell of this man as the safest place I'd ever known.

He whispers in my ear, "It means I think you've let yourself hurt more than you needed to."

I need to hear the words. They outrage me. But I also feel his expert lips on my earlobe, then on the sensitive flesh of my neck, and his warmth against my body. I try to protest, but before I can get the words out his mouth is on my own, and I dissolve into his gallant kiss. His mouth is cool, and fresh as always. No matter what he eats, it always seems that Ivan has just brushed his teeth. I've never loved kissing anyone the way I love kissing him.

The bell dings again.

"We're here," he says, still kissing me as he pushes me out the door into the hallway. His hands are all over me as we trip down the hall in a fit of kisses. He leads me to a room, opens it with his key card, and we enter the suite.

I gasp a little when I see the sumptuous carpets, rich cantaloupe shade of paint on the walls, with mint green crown molding. The fringed sofas and the ornate upholstery. Gorgeous.

"This way," he says, taking me through the exquisite living room area to the bathroom.

"What are you doing?" I ask.

Ivan brings me to the side of a large Jacuzzi bathtub. The floor is new, but done in an old style with pentagonal white and black tiles. He bends down to turn on the water, feeling it with his hand to make sure the temperature is just right. Have I mentioned lately how much I love this man's hands?

"What does it look like I'm doing?" he asks with a mischievous smile.

"It looks like you're going to take a bath."

"We're going to take a bath," he corrects me. Then, as the water runs, he stands and kisses me again, this time his fingers begin to slip the soft black fabric of the dress over my shoulders, and then past my waist, and down, until the damn thing is off.

"I shouldn't be doing this," I groan.

"Yes you should, baby," he says as he unfastens my bra, and expunges it with his deft, agile fingers. "You absolutely should." Next, the panties. He slips them down and off like he was removing the skin of a boiled tomato. It's all so natural and easy for this man, peeling women.

I now stand completely nude, and Ivan is still wearing all of his clothes. I have never felt so exposed. I am quite aware of the large, full-length mirror on the wall next to me. I try not to look at it, and Ivan, being Ivan, immediately notices this. He turns my body so that I face the mirror.

"I don't want to," I protest.

"Yes you do."

"It's not smart." I look away from myself.

"Shh," he says. The tub is only one-quarter full. "Look at her. Yourself, Zora. Look at yourself."

"Ivan, please." I don't want to look at myself, because I'm afraid if I do I'll realize how pathetic this is, how little respect I have for the woman in the mirror, and after all the years I've spent cultivating a very respectable version of myself for myself – on paper at least – it's just too painful to see myself this way.

"Just look at her." Gently, he turns my face toward my own reflection and I surrender control to him. I feel far too vulnerable, with him fully clothed next to me. I don't like it. But I love it at the same time. Hard to explain. He moves to stand behind me, and slips his hands around to cup my breasts. Slowly, I look up at our reflection. Besides the obvious mistake I am probably making by allowing this man access to a body that should have been deemed off limits to him long ago for his repeated failures to respect the soul housed within it, I realize I am not half bad, for a woman with a grown daughter. I blush at the sight of my own curves.

"Who would believe this was the toughest woman in the sports business," says Ivan as he toys with my nipples. They go from soft to erect in no time flat. He knows exactly what to do with them, always has. I pull a corner of my lower lip into my mouth, and bite it a little. Oh, Jesus, that feels good.

The tub is now half full.

Ivan continues to strum my breasts, jiggling them, pinching them, gentle and then aggressive, alternating like that, until the sensation moves through my nervous system to the center of my body – and lower. I don't want to, but I moan.

"I hate this," I say. "You. I hate you."

Ivan pinches my nipples harder still. "No you don't," he says as I moan once more.

"I do too," I insist. "I hate that you're so good at this."

"That makes no sense, baby," he says. He releases one breast and slides the free hand down my belly. I watch as he slips his hand between my legs, touching gently, teasing, moving near the sensitive spot, very near, then moving away, all while kissing my upper back. He does this on purpose. Toys with me. I think it's his life's mission. I want him so much. I want more than he's giving.

Three quarters full.

Suddenly, Ivan releases me, steps away and begins to remove his own clothes. I watch. He is perfectly built, muscular but not overly so, with just the right amount of hair on his chest. He has matching tattoos of razor wire wrapped around each of his biceps. As he drops his pants, I stare. This body is so familiar to me, and yet so strange. It's been a while. He is, of course, ready to go.

"Come here," he says as he takes a seat on the edge of the tub. Almost full now.

I do as he says. When I get next to him, he puts his hand around himself and looks at me with the little boy grin. I know what he wants. He doesn't have to say a word. I ease myself down to my knees, and take him in my mouth. He lets out a small sound, and as I work on him the sound of the water stops. I open my eyes, and see Ivan's got one hand on the faucet and one hand on my head.

"Time to get wet," he says, pulling my head up. I stand. Ivan also stands, and trades places with me, pulling me to sit exactly where he's been. "This kind of wet." He spreads my legs with his hands, kneels before me, and returns the favor. I tremble as he does this. Shock waves ride through my body. He uses his fingers, his tongue, both at the same time. He sticks his fingers deep inside of me, takes them out and brings them up to my own mouth, tracing my lips with my own juices. The man is incredibly nasty, and I don't know why I like it. Part of me doesn't like it at all, but part of me has always been thrilled by his willingness to experiment. Another part of me wonders which of his many other lovers he learned this stuff from, or how many women he's practiced on. Then, just as I'm about to climax, he stops.

"Get in the tub," he says.

I don't know why I do everything this man tells me to do. I follow the order, relinquish all power to this man. He joins me. He unwraps the bar of soap in the soap dish, and starts to lather me up. His hands sliding across my body are electric. I long to hold him, to kiss in an embrace, and we do, for a little while. Soon, though, Ivan has turned me around, and has me kneeling in the tub, my hands on the sides. He enters me from behind, and begins to drill me.

That's the only way I can describe it – a good, hard, fast-moving dance we've done many times before. This is his favorite position. No eye contact.

Afterward, I want to linger in the tub, hug, talk. I need some reassurance that I've not just made a terrible mistake. I also want us to hurry up and get dressed again so we don't miss the ballet.

But Ivan has other plans.

He's up, drying himself off and yawning.

"I'm so tired," he says. "Let's just go to bed. We'll catch the ballet another time."

He says it all as if I were annoying to him now. Ah, yes. This is familiar, too. After sex, when we were married, he'd always want to fall asleep, preferably alone in his own bed, while I'd be ready to go for a ten-mile jog. I dry off with him and together we crawl into bed. Soon, he's snoring with his back to me. Gone is the adoring Ivan who can't get enough of me. I am still wide awake when his cell phone rings in his pants pocket across the room.

"Ivan," I say, trying to rouse him. But he's out cold. I know I shouldn't do this, but I get up, tiptoe to the phone, and look at the name on the caller ID: Yvette Rollins. Who's Yvette Rollins? His teammate's girlfriend. Ice fills my veins. I go into the bathroom, close the door, and answer it.

"Hello?"

The girl at the other end sounds confused for a moment, but then she asks for Ivan. I lie, say I'm his assistant and that he's left his cell phone at his house. She's quiet for a moment.

"But he used it from Houston today to call me," she says.

"And you are?"

"This is Yvette. His fiancé. Is this really his assistant? You don't sound like her."

I don't know what to say, so I tell her the truth. "You're right. I'm his ex-wife, Zora Jackson. I just had sex with him. I wish I hadn't. I'm sorry. He mentioned you today. You like interior design?"

She is silent, so I continue.

"He said you were the girlfriend of a teammate of his. You picked this hotel, the Icon, right?"

She says in a choked-up voice, "You're lying. You're not at the Icon."

"I wish I were lying," I say. Now it's me who starts to choke up. I don't want to be here. Not now.

"He asked me to marry him last month," says Yvette. "He would never sleep with one of his ex-wives after that kind of commitment. I'm going to have him report his phone stolen."

I think of all the things I'd like to tell her, all the warnings I would like to give. But none of them come out.

She'll learn. In time. In time she'll realize Ivan is a liar, she'll realize he's not worth the time.

"You're right, Yvette, I am lying. I'm crazy. I stole Ivan's cell phone. I just didn't want him to marry you. That better?"

I hear her sniffling.

"Goodbye, Yvette. Good luck."

I end the call. Then I catch a glimpse of myself in the mirror. Naked, devastated, raw, a peeled tomato, skinless, feeling everything acutely, intensely, and everything is pain. She'll learn, I tell myself. Then again, I think, maybe she'll never learn. Some of us never do. I never did, apparently. I still haven't figured it out. I have a strange urge to call the cheerleader, to confess to her what a wreck I am, to warn her: Don't be like me.

Welcome back, Zora, I think as I shove my disappointed self back into my rumpled, damp black date dress. It seems so sort of pitiful and filthy now. Used up. Just like me. Welcome back to Life According to Ivan Barbosa, and don't let the door hit you in the ass on your way out.

Welcome the fuck back.

Mackenzie

The photographer wraps up his presentation, and Justin and I stand to leave amid the rumble of a satisfied crowd coming apart. I feel like a complete and total dork, but I take one of the programs from the event up to the photographer to have him sign it. I've never been this excited to meet someone in my life, mostly, I realize, because he is a lot like what I'd like to be like. The whole thing Zora talked about. She is so totally wise. I want to listen to her again.

"She's a photojournalist, too," Justin tells him as he distractedly signs the glossy paper.

"Really?" The photographer smiles at me and for the first time I can think of, I don't feel fraudulent.

"Yes," I say as I adjust my shoulders to be a little more like Zora's - up and proud. "But I hope one day to be as good as you."

"Thanks," he says.

Justin and I walk out into the humid darkness. "So," he says. "I don't really feel like going home yet."

"Me neither," I say. "I just want to talk about photography all night. Isn't that weird?"

"Not at all. You hungry?"

I shrug, even though the answer is yes. I am hungry. I'm always hungry. I long ago stopped answering that question honestly. "Not really," I say.

"Would you mind going to this great little Vietnamese restaurant?"

Vietnamese? The kind of food Dino refused to even try?

"Is it far?" I ask

"No. You follow me, okay?"

I practically skip along next him. "Sure."

"You look happy," he says.

I don't say anything. I feel happy. And confused.

As I drive to the restaurant, I call Zora Jackson, to tell her how much she helped me earlier in the day. I was raised to send thank-you cards, and to express gratitude when it is due.

"Miss Mackenzie," she says when she answers. She sounds a little sad. "Just thinkin' about you, oddly enough."

"Zora. Am I catching you at a bad time?"

"No. What's up?" It sounds like her nose is stuffed up a little.

"Well, first I just want to say I'm sorry for earlier today. I was really out of line, and it was so weird I hope it doesn't get in the way of us becoming friends."

"I've seen much weirder. Not a problem."

I say, "Okay, so remember what you said about being direct in life?"

"Uh huh."

"I'm going to be direct."

"You've found an indirect way of telling me this, but go ahead."

"I am totally going to break off my engagement to Dino." I hear my own voice as I say this, and it sounds like I've won the lottery or something.

"Oh?"

"He doesn't get me. I mean, he thinks he does, but he completely doesn't really know me. I mean, part of that is my fault because I haven't been totally honest with him, like about all kinds of things. But I know that if I was honest with him he wouldn't like me anymore, and I don't feel like spending my whole life, my whole married family life kind of a thing, with a guy I have to lie to about everything and everyone I am all the time. I hope that makes sense."

"So far."

"And I just found a guy who does."

"A guy who makes sense?"

"A guy who gets me. He's a stock boy at my aunt's tiny little dumpy market. I had to tell someone about him, and you're the only person I know who won't try to put me in a loony bin for it."

"Where?"

"A loony bin."

"No, I heard that part. Where's your aunt's market?"

"Magnolia Park. It's like this barrio in East Houston."

"Ah. Did you just say he's a stock boy?"

"Only not just a stock boy. He's a writer, and he's got this incredible sense of humor and he's nice and he likes my photographs. He's writing for a local paper and he's still in school but I think he's a really, really good writer and someday he wants to be a journalist just like I do. So right there you can see that he'd totally understand me. He thinks I'm good, and he totally respects that this is something I might want to do when I'm all done with cheerleading and pageants, and the most amazing thing about it is that this guy doesn't think I'm totally crazy for wanting to take pictures for a living. Everyone else I know except my Aunt Rosie thinks I'm crazy."

"Take a deep breath."

"Justin, that's the guy. He totally thinks I can do the photo thing with the Chronicle, and I'm thinking maybe if he believes in me I might not actually suck. And this is going to sound completely and totally insane – but I've been thinking a lot about what I need in life, like what I need to be totally happy, and do you know what I came up with?"

"No idea."

"A camera, a job taking pictures, traveling, and some comfortable clothes. That's really it. That's all I want. I've been doing pageants since I was six months old, Zora, and I have to tell you I am sick of dressing up and I am sick of makeup and all of that, and I know that you don't stay young forever. I mean, I don't think I'm old or anything, but I don't want to think of myself as a forty-year-old woman missing her best days because they're all behind her now. That's sort of pathetic. If I was a photojournalist, I could still be doing my best work at forty, or fifty, or sixty. At least for right now that's all I want. Money for film and all that. But I don't need a lot."

"Uh-huh."

"And I know everyone is going to think I'm totally crazy for doing this, but I feel like it's the right thing to do. I'm going to go down to Austin for the state championship next week and then I'm going to tell Dino I don't want to marry him. My mom is going to die, but I don't care anymore. Thanks to you, your example, I can't live my life for her anymore. I don't think I want to be married to a big-shot athlete."

"Uh-huh."

"I mean, I'm sure it would be this glamorous life and everyone would think I was so great because I was married to Dino. But it would be all about Dino, and I don't think I want my life to be all about Dino, you know? I think a life

209

that was all about some professional athlete instead of a life that was all about me would be a waste of a life, you know what I mean?"

Zora doesn't say anything, but I can hear her taking a deep breath. She blows the air out into the phone. "Miss Mackenzie, you have no idea how much I needed to hear what you have just told me."

"You?"

"I wish someone had told me this twenty years ago. Or even twenty-four hours ago, actually."

I have no idea what she means, and I don't think it would be polite to ask.

"So you don't think I'm making a total mistake that I'm going to live to regret? You don't think this is completely insane?"

"You have to be with someone who will be just as interested in respecting and admiring you as you are interested in respecting and admiring him. You can't be with a man because you admire him. You have to be with a man because he respects you and you respect him and it's fair."

"But here's the weird part, Zora. I don't think I want to get married."

"You just told me that."

"No, I don't just mean to Dino. I mean ever. I don't think I ever want to get married."

"That's not so weird, Mackenzie."

"Seriously. I think it might be cool not to, to just have this life where I'm going to exotic places, taking photos of events and people, publishing them in newspapers around the world and letting people know about important stuff, so that then people might be moved to take action."

"Girlfriend, it's a little bit late over here, and I've had a really rough night."

"I'm sorry. I didn't even think to ask you about your night."

"That's okay because I'm too raw to talk about it anyway."

"I'm sorry."

"Call me tomorrow, Mackenzie. I'm happy you made a decision you can live with. I wish I could say the same."

We say our goodbyes, and I hang up confused. Zora sounded down, and like she was disappointed in herself. How is that possible? I really hope it totally has nothing to do with what happened between us today. I'll have to find out more about this, but not right now. Right now I want to believe that the breakup with Dino that I am going to make happen tomorrow is already valid. I want to live as the new Mackenzie de la Garza, a woman on her own – or soon to be on her own, once I move out of my parents' house. A woman on the first day of the rest of her life, about to have dinner with a man who makes her happy.

I follow Justin's car into the parking lot of the Vietnamese restaurant. It's right downtown, near an underpass, and it look like several homeless men have camped out in the parking lot. I park the Liberty and wait for Justin to park his car and join me. I don't feel terribly safe walking around here alone, even though I work in Magnolia Park every single day. Nighttime in downtown Houston is another story.

As we walk toward the restaurant, a couple of the homeless men approach, asking for money. They look terrible and ragged, and my heart hurts for them. I hate the impotence I feel when I see the poverty in this city. There is so much of it. In a city with so much wealth, it seems patently unfair to me that these men should have nothing. One of the men drops to his knees when we ignore him, a hat in his hands.

"Please," he calls. "Look, I dropped to my knees. I'm begging here. I'm hungry."

Justin reaches into his pocket and pulls out a dollar bill, hands it to the man.

"God bless you," says the man.

I remember the last time I saw a homeless man with Dino. He shoved the man out of the way and told me most of the homeless in Houston are faking it, that they all have lots of money and choose to live this way to scam people. I didn't know what to say to him then. I'd wanted to help the men, but I was worried that Dino would have argued about it.

"That was nice of you," I tell Justin as he opens the large red door of the restaurant for me.

"He needs it more than I do," he says, shrugging.

As we walk to our table, I feel myself slipping the engagement ring off my finger and delicately depositing it in the front pocket of my jeans. I feel instantly lighter. I smell the lemongrass and ginger in the air, and decide I'm going to eat. I'm going to sit down at this table here with this kind, attractive man, and I'm going to discuss photography, journalism and life – and I'm going to eat.

As Justin holds my chair, waiting for me to get into it so he can scoot me toward the table, I surprise him by spontaneously planting a kiss on his cheek.

"Whoa," he says, grinning.

I look at him, and don't resist the urge to do it again, this time on the lips. Just a quick, sweet little peck.

"What was that for?" he asks.

"Just because."

"Oh. Okay. In that case-"

He leans toward me and kisses me this time, and it lasts a bit longer. I get tingles everywhere. I want to do it again, but the waiter is looking a little uncomfortable by now.

I sit, and he scoots me in before going to his side of the table and sitting down.

"Not to ruin the mood," he says. "But what about Dino, your betrothed?"

"I don't want to marry Dino."

"Why not? I mean, not that I'm upset about that or anything."

"I'm not in love with him."

"Does he know?"

I shake my head. "I'll tell him next time I see him."

Justin looks at his menu. "Could you wait to do that whole breaking up thing until I'm safely out of the country? I'd appreciate it if you could do that, because, and I think you'll agree with me on this, I'm really too young to die. And I'm much too weak to fight back. Unless you help me. But even then. You're not a large woman, I don't know if you've noticed that."

"I won't tell him about you."

"I mean, you could. If you wanted to. But if you think it would be cool if I lived long enough for us to have another non-date that turned into a weird thing where you're kissing me in the middle of a Vietnamese restaurant that's really good but happens to be in a bad part of town."

"That sounds fun."

"Would you let me take you out on one of those again, Mackenzie? Like, next weekend. I could take you out next weekend for a non-date that could end with us at some weird hole-in-the-wall restaurant with you kissing me again."

"Okay," I say. "Excellent."

I should feel guilty about this, all of it, but the truth is, I don't.

The truth is, I feel free.

Zora

I am standing on the front steps of my townhouse waiting for the late driver – I will never use this car service again, I swear to God – to come to take me to the airport for my flight to New York when Yardbird pulls up in a souped-up vintage Ford Mustang, with Miles Davis blasting. It's got a motor that thunders like a buffalo stampede right here in my slender little driveway.

I make as annoyed a face as I can manage, continue to hold with the car company on my phone as he exits his car and approaches me. Lissette is at school, so I know with a degree of certainty that the boy didn't come to see her. Best to pretend he did, though.

"She's not here," I tell him as I turn away from him. "You can run on home now."

"She's right in front of me," he says. "How you doing?"

The woman on the other end of the line finally comes off hold and tells me that there is no record of me having ordered a car for this afternoon, which is completely insane because I just got the call an hour ago asking for directions. We start to bicker and I'm starting to lose my temper. I find myself screaming into the phone, "I have a plane to catch, and I'm already going to be late as it is. Forget it. Okay, just cancel the fucking order and I'll get a cab."

I end the call and shake my head.

"Hey," says Yardbird. "I can take you somewhere. You need to go to the airport, I can take you."

I consider this. I look at his car. "I didn't bring earplugs," I say.

"Its not that bad inside."

I follow him to the car and allow the young man to open the passenger side door for me. I am surprised to find the inside of the car clean and refurbished. He also has one of the finest car stereos I have ever seen.

"Nice ride," I tell him as he backs the car onto the street.

"Thanks. See? Can barely hear the engine now."

He flips on the stereo and presses past the Miles album he was listening to when he pulled up and stops on an album I thought no one but me liked anymore. Charles Mingus. I find my shoulders relaxing with the comforting, familiar sounds, and I hum a little bit of the melody.

"You know this song?" asks Yardbird, surprised.

"Of course I know this song."

I feel his eyes on me. "It just keeps getting better," he says.

"Great music does that."

"Not the music. You. The whole package, it just keeps getting better. The more I get to know you, the more I like you. It's usually the opposite way around with the women I meet."

I look directly at him this time. "Look. I'd like you to stop talking like that. Right now. I'm thirty-six years old, Yardbird. That's a whole twelve years older than you. I don't need that kind of complication in my life and God knows you don't."

"Age ain't nothing but a number," he says.

I laugh at the cliché. "Please, child. Don't give me that."

"What are you afraid of, Zora?"

"Nothing."

"You think I'm ugly?"

"No."

"You think I'm too poor? My parents are pretty well off, actually, and I have a bit of a trust fund, so if you think this is all about me romancing you for cash you can forget that shit right now. I'm paid. I'm taken care of already."

"That's not the problem," I say.

"Then please tell me before I go crazy trying to figure you out what the problem is, because from where I'm sitting there's no problem to be found."

I sigh, and tell it like it is. "The problem is that men are programmed to be ruthless and deceitful in their youth, Yardbird. I have had enough of that shit in my life to last me four lifetimes, and I'm not about to go jump into another situation where that is likely to happen to me."

"So you think that just because a man is young he's going to be a dog? Is that what you're saying?"

"That's exactly what I'm saying."

"Let me ask you something. I been reading about the personal problems your ex-husband is going through. He's all grown up now, or at least he's old enough to be all grown. And do you think he's outgrown his dog behavior?"

I think about last night, and will myself not to cry. "No."

"Okay. So that right there tells me your theory is dead wrong. That, and the fact that I am twenty-four years old and I've never cheated on a woman in my life."

"Never?"

"Zora, why would I do something stupid like that?"

"Because that's what men do."

"Who the hell told you that shit?"

"People. Life. Experience."

"Well, then I'd say you need to meet some new people, live a little more, and have a different kind of experience."

"That what you think?"

"It's what I know. Listen to me. I'm not a dog. I have never been a dog, and I will never be a dog. Do you want to know why? It's because dogs don't change. And good men don't change. You cannot go from being a member of the dog team to being a member of the good guy team. It don't work like that. Values don't suddenly show up when a man reaches a certain age. They're built into his character by his parents and his upbringing."

I stare out the window at the freeway, and the ever-present construction on the freeway, and realize that this very young man has just made a very solid argument on a very basic point. A point I should have figured out on my own long ago but which escaped me, probably because of my own challenged upbringing.

"You could have a point," I tell him. "But that doesn't mean I think it's okay for me to get involved with a man twelve years younger than me."

"Why does that matter?"

"It just does. It's not part of the plan."

"The plan. You like plans, huh? You want to writes lists all the time and makes sure everything goes the way the list says, right?"

"Most of the time, yes. That's how I function best."

"Well I sure wouldn't want to mess up your nice, neat planned little world by being a good man who's falling for you or anything like that, if it's not in the plan."

"I appreciate that." I feel disappointed that he's seemingly gotten angry and given up so easily. He was actually finally starting to win me over.

"It's not terrible to be spontaneous now and then," he says. "But I can respect what you're saying and where you're coming from, and I know when I'm not wanted or welcomed. So I'll back off."

We don't talk for much of the rest of the drive, listening to the music. We get to the airport.

"What airline?" he asks me.

"American," I say.

"You going direct to New York?" he asks as he slides his cool car up to the curb. I nod and he asks me which airport. I tell him I'm flying into LaGuardia. "Well, Zora Jackson, wonder woman, I hope you have a nice, peaceful flight, and that once you get home you allow yourself to relax and enjoy this incredible life you've built for yourself."

"Thanks," I say. I open the door and step out, a sentence unspoken on my tongue. I close the door, but before he has a chance to drive away I open it again and say, "You know, you gave up a lot faster than I thought you would, after all that fancy talking."

He smiles at me with renewed energy. "Yeah? You think I might have given up too soon?"

"Maybe," I say as flirtatiously as I can. Then I close the door. He squeals off in a peal of tires that remind me of exactly how unseasoned he really is.

Forty minutes later, as I'm settling into my First Class window seat – with no one sitting next to me, thank God! – I look up at the people who have begun to board for coach. I hate the way they have to walk through First Class and how they look at you all like you think you're better than them or something. I read a magazine and try to ignore them. But then I hear someone whistling the tune to the Mingus song Yardbird and I were just listening to in the car. I look up, and there he is, boarding my God damned plane.

"What the hell do you think you're doing?" I cry. Everyone who has heard me turns to stare at me, including the flight attendant, who looks more than a little worried. These days you have to be very careful what you say on an airplane or in an airport. If you sound too angry they're likely to think you're some kind of terrorist, especially if you happen to have darker skin, which both Yardbird and I do.

"Thought I'd try a little spontaneity of my own," says Yardbird.

"Don't you have school?"

"I have a class tomorrow that I can miss, and then the whole weekend basically off. I would love to spend some time at Sweet Basil and the Museum of Natural History."

The line has started to move.

"Talk to you when we get there, sister," he says, and he winks at me.

Winks at me.

I resist the urge to turn and stare at him, and return to my magazine. Soon, we are airborne, and I can't stop smiling with the knowledge that Yardbird is somewhere on this airplane, flying discreetly and directly into my too-closed, lonely little world.

Mackenzie

The morning of the state competition I wake before dawn to find my mother already up, with a healthy breakfast of plain oatmeal and banana slices on the table for me. She's still in her silky robe and pajamas, and her eyes bear the traces of yesterday's mascara. Nonetheless, she is completely focused on me, in an adoring way that feels unfamiliar and strange. I don't know what to make of my mother when she's not criticizing me. For example, as I sip coffee at the table she sits across from me and leans her chin into her hand, elbow on the table, a silly smile playing across her face.

"What?" I ask. "Why are you looking at me like that?" Even though "that" is lovingly. The way a mother is supposed to look at her children, I believe.

"It's just I can't believe my daughter is going to get married. It's amazing."

Now would be a good time to tell her I don't plan to marry Dino, I think, but I don't want to risk having a blowout fight that might make me miss the bus to Austin. My girls are counting on me, and I need this day to be as stress-free as possible. Today, I need to focus on my girls winning.

"So that's why you're smiling at me like that?" I ask her. "Because I'm going to marry Dino? I thought you might, you know, be happy that I'm about to take my girls to state."

My mother nods like a happy child. "Never in my wildest dreams did I think we'd end up that rich or that famous." It seems like she has completely missed the last half of what I just told her. Like she doesn't realize I'm about to take my kids to the most important competition of the year.

"So this isn't about state?" I ask.

My mother shakes her head. "I'm sure those girls will do fine, and even if they don't it's not the end of the world."

"Ah," I say. It wouldn't be the end of her world. It would be the end of theirs, though.

"I'm just so tickled you're going to marry Dino," she says. "I couldn't be happier, Mackenzie. All my hard work to make you a perfect little lady has paid off." She smiles until it looks like her eyes might pop.

I shrug and try to manage a return smile. It's fake, and I'm sure she can tell it's fake. But my mother has never had a problem with fake smiles.

It's honest disagreement - and disobedience - she can't tolerate.

I get to Mariposa High school at seven in the morning, just as some taggers scurry off through a weedy lot across the street, and find several of my girls already huddled at the north end of the parking lot waiting for the bus. We are scheduled to leave in half an hour. The bus isn't here yet, so I get on the cell phone and call the charter company to make sure it's on the way. The girls held God-knows-how-many car washes to raise the money for this bus, and we're not about to be let down. The dispatcher at the bus company tells me the bus is en route. Relieved, I lock up my car, gather my belongings, and join my girls on the sidewalk. We hug, and I notice the nervous energy in their eyes.

At exactly seven-twenty the bus pulls into the lot. All of the girls are here, and they pile on in an orderly way. Three moms have agreed to come with us, including Samantha's mother. I sit with her near the front of the bus. Once everyone is settled in, I give them a little pep talk, set the rules of conduct for the three-hour ride to Austin, and off we go.

I spend the first hour of the ride reading through the Houston Chronicle, which has a nice package on the state cheerleading contest and even mentions us as a leading contender for the first-place prize, and chatting with the mothers. Soon, Rosie calls on my cell phone to wish me luck at the competition. I almost cry.

"Thank you," I say.

"I know you're going to do great. You always do."

After a while I hang up, and listen as Samantha's mother talks about the elaborate Sweet Fifteen the family has planned for her daughter. Her admiration and love for her child is obvious in the proud lift of her head and the detailed description of the dress and catering she has planned. I cringe to realize she sounds a lot like my own mother planning my wedding, and I consider talking to her about planning for her daughter to go to college, too. But I've tried that once before with this woman and it didn't work. I don't know any other way to communicate to her the importance of an education in a young American woman's life, especially when it seems like she still sees her daughter as little more than someone's future husband. There's too much of that going around, I think as I watch the suburbs gradually melt into grassy fields. Too totally much of it. Instead of wasting my energy trying to convince this woman of something she will never likely believe, I turn my attention to the speech I plan to give Dino later tonight, after the competition, over a late dinner. It won't be easy, but I bet it's going to feel really, really good.

The bus drops us off at a budget motel on the outskirts of Austin, and the chaperones and I make sure the girls get settled in their rooms before heading to our own to unpack. It's not the kind of hotel I usually stay in when I travel with my parents. They favor 5-star hotels, suites. This particular place seems to have cigarette burns in every comforter, and paper cups in the bathrooms instead of the glasses I'm used to. The girls seem impressed, though. They gasp and giggle with the thrill of having rooms of their own – two girls to a room, actually. They grab the TV remotes and brag about the free cable. To them, this is a luxury vacation.

After unpacking and relaxing for two hours with a photo book (Dino called once, but I ignored him) I grab a couple of the moms and we head to a Wendy's and load up on baked potatoes, salads, diet sodas and hamburgers for the girls. We bring them back and hand them out with instructions to eat, relax for an hour, shower, change, get their hair and makeup done, and then meet up in front of the hotel to get the us to the Gregory Gymnasium on the Univ. of Texas campus. The competition began early this morning, but we're not scheduled to perform until mid-afternoon. Some of the girls wanted to head over early to see the other teams, but I told them I thought that was a bad idea. I think it's best for them to relax and to think of themselves as the only team in the world that matters. And more than anything, I remind the girls, I want them to remember to have fun with this. To take it seriously but not so seriously they forget the point, which is fun.

We arrive at the gym with forty minutes to spare. As the bus pulls to a stop, out the window we see gangs of young women in cheerleader outfits walking here and there, and no shortage of college boys who've decided to come hang out. I stand in the aisle and face my girls. They look confident, excited, and just the tiniest bit nervous. This is exactly how I want them to look.

"Okay, girls," I say. "Deep breath. You own this place. Remember that. You belong here. You know this routine inside and out, and you have performed it flawlessly under much harsher conditions than what we're about to find inside that gym. I believe in you, I love you, and I have total faith in all of you to succeed. You ready?"

"Ready!" they cry.

With that, we exit the bus, and walk with large, confident strides up the steps and through the door. The stadium is completely packed, with other teams, their families, the press, and spectators. Heads turn at the sight of us, and people begin to whisper. Some of them already know who we are. And by the end of this day I am absolutely certain they all will.

The girls follow me to the registration table, where I sign them in and hand the organizers the CD of our music. Then we find our assigned warmup spot on the gym floor. I lead the girls through some large, rhythmic movements to loosen them up, and then some stretches. I count them through the routine, asking them to visualize it, but do not ask them to perform it. There's no need for that. Creative visualization is far more effective in getting them psyched without using precious energy. I check their hair and makeup. They look perfect.

I lead them across the floor to the holding area for the next team, and here they catch their first glimpse of the competition. It's a school from Waxahachie, outside of Dallas, performing well to Christian pop.

After the Waxahachie team leaves the floor, it is swept and readied for us. I stand the girls in a circle, and we join hands. I lead them through a quick prayer, and then our name is called. I walk to the sidelines as my girls take the floor. They do as I've instructed them to, and smile directly at the judges, never once sneaking a look at me. They know I've got their backs. They know I'm their biggest fan.

"Next up, ladies and gentlemen, the Mariposa High School Matadors!"

I feel my pulse quicken and will my hands out of the fists they find themselves in. I breathe deeply. Soon I hear the clicks counting off the song, and then there it is, our dance number, blasting through the speakers. The girls burst to life, and begin to kick, jump, twist and twirl their way through the routine without missing a step. They add the flourish and attitude we are known for, and they completely, absolutely burn the thing up. They look so professional, so in tune. I hold my breath, count through the moves with them. The complete and total thrill of watching them is almost too much for me to take. I hear the crowd roar when the girls pull off some of their trickier stunts, and I hear them roar again when the girls move through the samba, salsa and merengue moves I've taught them. Breathe, Mackenzie, I tell myself. Breathe.

Before I know it, the song has ended and the girls stop dead still at exactly the right moment. I cannot believe it was that good. I knew they'd kick ass, but I didn't realize they'd kick that much ass. The crowd is elated, and I turn to see everyone in the stands rising to their feet. The judges shake their heads, impressed, trying not to show how blown away they are by these girls. The girls see it, and they know what they've just done here. We wait, all of us, as the score is calculated and posted on the scoreboard above the crowd. All eyes turn toward the numbers, and we wait. Then, there it is. A perfect score. A perfect score. In all my years of coaching and competing I have never seen a perfect score.

The girls begin to jump and scream and hold one another, and I run out to join them.

"Y'all did it!" I cry, real tears streaming down my face. "You did it! You did it!" Next thing I know, the girls have lifted me onto their shoulders. Only when we've gone back to the sidelines and the reporters come rushing over to talk to me do they set me down.

As we walk up the steps into the stadium to take our seats to wait for the final teams to compete, I step aside and return the call from my mother. What could possibly be this important that she has to interrupt me now? She knows how important this competition is to me.

"Mom," I say when she answers. "This better be important. I'm in the middle of the competition."

She sounds congested, like she's been crying. "I'm sorry to bother you. But it's Rosie. She's in the hospital."

"What? What happened?"

"Apparently she's had breast cancer for the past year and never bothered to tell any of us about it," says my mother. "She collapsed at the store this morning and was rushed her to the hospital. I just got the call from your grandma right before I called you, and the doctor told her that the cancer had spread and metastasized through her whole body."

I feel the room spin. The noise of the crowd, so happy minutes ago, is nothing but noise now. "How bad is it?" I ask.

My mother sobs. "I should have been better to her, you know that? I shouldn't have been so hard on her."

"Mom. How bad is it?"

"Grandma said the doctor told her Rosie might not live more than a month."

"Oh my God."

"I can't believe this."

"Why didn't she tell anyone?" I ask.

"Your grandmother said Rosie didn't want anyone to worry."

"I'll be home as soon as I can," I tell her.

"We're on our way to the hospital to see her now," my mother tells me. "You stay and do what you need to do. I just thought you'd want to know."

"I can try to get the moms to take over getting the girls back to Houston. I can get a bus back home or something."

"Why don't you ask Dino to bring you home?"

I think carefully about what I'm going to say. My mother is already devastated. I shouldn't add misery to her life. "He has practice, mom. I can't just ask him to leave. I'll see what I can do."

I try to find enough air to fill my lungs, but for some reason it feels like all the air in the world has suddenly disappeared.

Zora

I exit the plane almost as soon as the door is opened, and take a seat in the gate area. As the other passengers deplane I try to look busy by checking my phone. Seventeen new email messages? Twelve texts? Ten new voicemail messages? We were only in the air for three and a half hours. Damn.

I peek up at the thread of people snaking out of the doorway. Not Yardbird. Still not Yardbird. What's he doing? Toying with me? I continue to wait, until it seems every last person has gotten off of the damn plane, and then, there he is. Tall, dark and handsome, with a playful look in his eyes. He walks over to me and takes the seat next to mine without a word.

"You enjoy your flight?" I ask.

"A little bumpy at the beginning, but sometimes that's a sure sign of smooth sailing ahead."

"You trying to be cute?" I ask.

"Yes."

I look at my watch. "I have to go." I stand up. He stands with me. I walk down the concourse, and he walks alongside me, whistling. I take the escalator to the baggage claim area, and he's right behind me.

I find Alvin, my usual driver, greet him with a handshake, and along tags Yardbird, standing at my side.

Alvin looks at me with a question in his eye, and the question seems to involve Alvin wondering whether he ought to kick this man's ass for bothering me.

I shake my head and say, "It's okay," even though I'm still not sure it is.

Alvin, discreet and professional, turns and begins to walk out of the building.

"Just what do you think you're doing?" I hiss at Yardbird as he trails me out the door and toward the waiting Towncar.

"I hope I'm coming with you."

"Did I invite you?"

"No. But I was hoping that by the time we got to the car you might."

Alvin holds the door open for me, averts his eyes and tries not to notice that I'm being followed by a younger man. Yardbird waits on the curb with a sincere, decent, honest face, his brows lifted hopefully, uncertainly. I think about what might happen to him if I left him here. He'd get a cab, find a way to waste some time. He'd go back home. I think about how I'd feel if Yardbird went back home. I wouldn't feel good.

"Get in," I say, pointing to the open door.

"Cool! For reals?" he asks, sounding for a moment very young and very naïve.

"For reals," I repeat.

He folds his long, lean body into the limo, and as I scramble in after him I can smell his dark, spicy cologne. It sends a thrill down my back, and I shiver as the door snaps shut behind me. I ignore it, of course, and secure my seatbelt. My eyes adjust to the darkness inside the car, and I can make out Yardbird's happy face.

"McCoy Tyner is playing at the Blue Note tonight," Yardbird tells me as Alvin slides into his seat and starts the engine.

"And?" I ask, trying to seem disinterested even though I love McCoy Tyner. Did this boy go through my entire record collection?

"And I was hoping to take you there. We could share some wine, hear some music, talk. Get to know each other."

I stare coldly at him, and try to visualize a wall between us. One of the many walls that have kept me relatively safe over the years. He flinches and leans away from me a little.

"Or," he says. "I could get me a hotel somewhere and get out of your hair for a while. Check with you in the morning when you're not so grumpy and tired."

"You think I'm grumpy and tired?" The wall falls away on it's own. I am not sure how, or why.

"Sure seems like it."

I lean forward. "Alvin, change in plans. Take us to the Blue Note."

"Yes, Miss Jackson."

I hesitate to look at Yardbird because I fear he'll gloat in his victory. When I do look at him, Yardbird looks pleased, but not in the competitive triumphant way Ivan might have been pleased in this kind of situation. Yardbird seems happy for me, happy with me, like he's happy – and even more than that, like he's grateful – that I've decided to have him around.

"Wow," I say.

"Wow what?"

"Wow, you're not rubbing your victory in my face," I say. I realize as I say it that it might not make sense, but Yardbird seems to understand instantly what I mean.

He says, simply: "That's that difference between musicians and athletes, Zora. This is what I've been trying to get you to understand about me."

I think about this. About how jazz has always appealed to me because of its collaborative nature, how it has always soothed me to listen to the respectful interplay between the men in jazz bands, especially after a day of dealing with the egos of athletes. I get goosebumps as the truth of what this young man has spoken hits me. I look at him and feel the layers of my fear of him starting to peel away.

Yardbird reaches out and softly touches me hand.

"May I?" he asks as he slips his fingers into mine. I nod, and say nothing. His eyes shine with respect, admiration, and peaceful understanding.

As the Towncar zips slightly too fast along Grand Central Parkway toward Manhattan, I realize with a shock that even with all my life experience and success, I have never, until this moment, known what it felt like to have a man look at me like that.

Mackenzie

I say goodbye to the girls at the hotel, explain the family emergency to them, leave them and their championship trophy in the capable hands of the team mothers.

I check out of the hotel, and the driver from Enterprise picks me up in my white rental Taurus. I drop him at the Enterprise rental location, sign the forms, and speed away as the clouds gather above the earth, dark and heavy.

As I drive away from Austin, the rain begins. I call Dino on my cell phone and tell him I won't be able to meet him for dinner. I tell him about Rosie.

"Huh. That sucks," he says flatly.

I wait to see what else he'll say, but silence meets me. That sucks? That's it? That is all he can find to say? He doesn't offer any other form of sympathy. I can't honestly tell if he thinks Rosie's illness sucks, or if he thinks missing dinner with me sucks, and I totally don't care enough to ask him.

"I'm sorry we're missing dinner because there's something else I have to tell you," I say.

"Yeah?" I can hear him chewing. Eating something. I hear the TV on in the background, with the sound of sports. "I have something to tell you, too. I wanted to tell you in person, because I know you'll be psyched, but whatever. At practice today there was a scout and he took me out after and told me I reminded him of Peyton Manning."

"Dino, please let me talk for a second?"

"Peyton Manning! I was, like, man, that's an incredible compliment. I mean, it's not the first time I heard it, I mean, you know, do you realize you're going to marry a man who's going down in history books as one of the best players in American football, ever? Doesn't that make you feel amazing, baby?"

"I want to break up."

As I say it, I realize he's talking, too. He has interrupted me. He keeps talking.

"You would have totally hated where we went, though. He took me to some strip club. So I don't want you acting all pissy 'cause I've been at a tittie bar."

"Didn't you hear what I just said?" I scream into the phone.

"Huh? You said something?"

"I said I want to break up with you, Dino! I don't want to marry you. I don't want any of this. I'm sick of it."

"What the fuck? I didn't get a lap dance or nothin'. Damn, girl. Calm the fuck down."

I sigh.   "I don't care if you go to a strip club. I hope you go to strip clubs! I hope you find a stripper to adore you. That's what you need. I'm breaking up with you because I don't love you and I don't think I ever did. I can't live a lie, Dino. I've been wanting to do this for a week. Actually, I never wanted to say yes to you. I just did it because I thought I had to."

Silence. Finally, Dino has nothing to say. At least for a few seconds. "You're fucking nuts," he says. "What is it, PMS or some shit?"

"No, it's not PMS. It's you, Dino."

He laughs. "What are you talking about, it's me? Do you not understand who I am? Do you not realize how many women would kill to be with me, and I picked you? Do you not understand how fucking lucky that makes you?"

"Do you not understand what I just said? I don't want to marry you. I am breaking up with you. I wanted to do it in person because I think it's totally tacky to break up with someone on the phone, but I don't have a choice because as we speak I'm driving like a maniac to get to my aunt's hospital room, which, by the way, you didn't even ask about and don't even care about. I mean, why the hell would any woman want to marry a man who hears that her aunt is dying and all he can think of to say is 'that sucks'? I mean seriously, Dino! That's pathetic!"

"Well what the hell do you want me to say?"

"I don't want you to say anything. Not anymore. I don't want to hear you! I don't want to have to teach you what to say at the right time. I don't want to have to coach

241

you in how to make me feel good, Dino. I don't think it should take that much work to be with a man."

"You're fucking crazy."

"Fine. If that's what you think, fine. I'm crazy. Okay, Dino? I'm the crazy girl who doesn't want to marry you. I'm crazy because I think that if I'm going to be with a man he better understand that what I do and what I think and what I feel are just as important as him and his feelings and thoughts and everything like that. I don't care if you think I'm crazy!"

"That's why you're going to end up alone like your crazy aunt."

"What?"

"Rosie. If she was married like a normal person you wouldn't have to rush back to take care of her."

"You're disgusting," I say.

"And you're going to end up just like her. Dying alone."

The words feel like a punch in the gut. "Fuck you, Dino. I like being alone, you know that? I actually like it. I like doing my photography, and I like thinking about things that honestly I don't think you'd even be able to understand half of."

"Yeah, whatever, loner. Like what?"

"Like poetry."

He starts to laugh. "Whatever, Mackenzie, okay? Whatever."

"Nicely put, Dino. Very eloquent."

"Whatever."

"Eloquent. Do you even know what the word means?'

"Yeah, well, you're a bitch."

"I'll mail you the ring."

"Fuck you."

"No, fuck you. Rosie is ten times the human being you'll ever be, no matter how much money you make and how many strip clubs some stupid asshole scout takes you to."

I am shocked to hear the profanity coming out of my mouth, but it feels good to express my true feelings.

"Keep the fucking ring. You'll need it, you know that? You'll need the money. Sell it and buy yourself a big box of Midol. Because whatever asshole you end up with next is going to need it."

"I'm hanging up now, Dino," I say, but he beats me to it.

Tears cloud my eyes. I blink them away as I end the call and toss the phone to the floor. There's nothing left to say to him. I wipe my eyes on my shoulders, stare at the long road ahead, and I cry. But it's not Dino I'm crying for.

It's Rosie.

Zora

The house lights go down, and a hush comes over the crowd. McCoy Tyner, one of the last living legends of the bebop era, a man who has played with John Coltrane, Joe Henderson, and everyone of importance in between, walks stoop-shouldered onto the stage, his body aged but his eyes still bright as they take in the crowd.

Yardbird sets his glass of wine down, scoots his chair back, and stands, clapping. Others do the same. I stand, too, a standing ovation for one of the most delicate, collaborative male minds to exist.

The pianist observes the crowd, and shakes his head like he can't believe we'd do this. Like life, in all its infinite grace, amuses him to no end. He laughs a little at us, and the other members of the trio come out. Tyner sits at the piano, stretches his long, graceful fingers, and with little more than a gentle nod to the others, begins to play.

The music is meditative, hypnotic, somehow circular and whole the way life is circular and whole. We take our seats again, and this time Yardbird moves his closer to mine. I sip the cool, mellow, dark red wine, feel his warmth next to me, and feel my body start to relax. I am like a dried old sponge suddenly submerged in water, softening at the edges, powerless to stop the change. Do you know how long it has been since I let myself relax? Since I let anything new soak past this skin? Since I felt so alive and in the moment as I do now? The phone is turned completely off in my bag, for the first time in years. I've sent Alvin home for the night with plans to take a cab. For the moment, I am a free woman, a woman softening into her own light, a woman listening to music that seems to me to be the freest in all the world, next to a man whose mere glance makes me feel understood.

I watch Yardbird. He closes his eyes and nods to the beat, a smile playing across his lips. As the tone of the music changes, so does his expression. His forehead wrinkles in thought, intense, and his whole head turns a little sideways like he's listening for a sound in the wind that is hard to pick out. When the music changes again, so too his body language. Yardbird is a man who doesn't just listen to music, he really hears it. He understands it for the language that it is. He feels it in every part of his being. It speaks to him, and his fierce intelligence at this moment speaks to me.

When the song ends, his eyes open, and seek me out. "Wow," he says. "These guys are incredible."

I reach out for his hand with my own, the wall between us gone. "I think you might be, too," I say. "As much as it scares me to say so."

Yardbird leans toward me and plants a small, delicate, thoughtful kiss on my lips. It feels as good as Ivan's kisses have felt. Better. Lord have mercy on me.

"Don't be scared anymore, Miss Zora," he says. "Ain't nothin' to be afraid of with me."

Mackenzie

I rush down the hall, looking at the numbers on the doors of the hospital rooms, seeking Rosie's. I see my mother first, however. She is seated outside the room, her head in her hands. My father paces the hall nearby, his cell phone to his ear. He speaks in hushed tones. My mother looks up as I approach, and scowls at me.

"How is she?" I ask.

"What is wrong with you?" she asks, standing and grabbing my arm. She pulls me away from the room.

"What are you doing?" I ask, afraid.

"Dino just called me," she says. Her fingers dig into the flesh of my arm.

"Ow, mom, stop it!" I pull away from her. "Stop making a scene."

"First, Rosie, and now this?" She is crying hard. "How could you do this to us?"

"To who, mom?"

"To me. To this family! To yourself. How could you?"

"I don't want to talk about this with you right now," I say. Adrenaline pours through my system. I have an urge to punch my own mother. I turn away from her and walk down the hall. She follows and tries to grab my arm again. This time, I spin toward her and grab her hand. "Don't touch me," I order her in a voice that is calmer than I feel. I shove her hand away. My mother stares at me, stunned. I have never stood up to her like this.

"I don't know you," she says. "I don't know who you are."

I leave her standing there, and rush toward my aunt's room. My father sees me and nods his hello, still on the phone. I duck into the room, and find Rosie surrounded by familiar faces from the neighborhood, including a familiar face that makes my heart beat faster. Justin is here.

Rosie looks up as I walk in. Her eyes seem sunken in dark holes. Her face is pale, pasty, and her lips look white and dry. I immediately notice her bald head. Of course. She's been wearing wigs this past year because she's lost her hair from the cancer treatments. She offers a weak smile, and says, "There's my girl. I was wondering where you'd been."

"Oh, Rosie!" The cry escapes my lips. I rush to her side. Justin moves from his seat near the head of the bed and gives it to me. He has tears in his eyes. I sit, and place my hand on her forehead.

"The pain," says Rosie.

"Why didn't you tell anyone?" I cry.

"Because I love you too much to let you worry about this," she says. Her voice is raspy, and she gulps and gurgles a bit with the effort of breathing. She rolls her eyes toward me and asks, "Have you had your internship interview?"

I tell her not yet.

"I want you to promise me..." Her voice trails off and she begins to hack and cough.

"Don't talk, Rosie, rest. It's okay," says Justin.

She finishes coughing. "Rest? For what? I'm not getting better."

"Don't say that!" I cry. My mother enters the room dabbing at her eyes. The thought that she is crying more from grief at me breaking off my engagement to Dino makes me hate her right now. I don't want her here. In many ways, Rosie has been more like a mother to me than my own mother.

"I'm sorry, Mackenzie," Rosie tells me. "I've made peace with it. You should, too."

"I won't!" I start to cry.

"Promise me," she continues. "That you will take that internship and you will follow your dream of taking photos around the world."

I look at her. The air rasps out of her lungs as her head falls heavily onto the pillow.

"When is your interview?" she asks.

"Wednesday," I say.

"Wednesday is the Miss Texas pageant," snaps my mother. "You can't do anything else that day."

Rosie's face grows tense as she seems to fight the pain.

"Promise me," she repeats, looking directly at me. "Do the right thing, Mackenzie. The right thing for your future. It's my official dying wish. You better not let me down. Tell me you'll go to that interview."

I look at my mother's tight face and angry scowl.

"I promise I'll go to the interview," I say.

"I want more than that," says Rosie. "Promise me that if you get the internship you'll take it."

"If I get the internship, I promise to take it," I say. I feel my mother's tension and disgust.

"Good girl," says Rosie, her face relaxing, and her eyes closing. "Now if you all don't mind I think I'm going to take a nap for a little while."

I feel a hand on my back, and turn to find my father at my side. I don't know when he snuck in. I look at him, at the warmth in his eyes.

"You're doing the right thing," he says softly. "Life is short, Mackenzie. Much too short."

Zora

It is Tuesday, and I wake up late. This is the fourth day in a row I've allowed myself to sleep in. I've canceled all my appointments for the week, called in sick to my own damn company, told myself the world will go on without me to micromanage it. I wake in the strong, sturdy arms of Yardbird Williams. The moment my eyes flutter open, his lips are there to kiss me. He's already awake, cradling me, being careful not to make too much noise. I get the feeling he's been watching me.

"Good morning, beautiful," he says.

With that, our bodies begin to move against each other, and we begin to make love again. His expression does not change the way Ivan's does during lovemaking. Unlike Ivan, Yardbird has no need to hide behind his dysfunctions in bed. He has no need to turn me into some kind of object to make love to me. He is the first and only man I have ever been with who seems to be making love to me as a human being and not just to be having sex with me as a woman. I can literally feel our souls meet and touch, and the power of it sets me off balance a little, and makes me cry tears of joy in the throes of passion.

Afterwards, we hold each other and he says, "I bet it will still feel like this twenty years from now. Thirty. When we're old and gray."

"I'm already old and gray. What the hell you talking about?"

He moves back from me and looks at me earnestly. "I mean it when I say I want this to last that long."

"Isn't it a little early in the game to be talking like that?"

He shakes his head and playfully messes up my hair. "Will you ever stop thinking of love as a sport?"

I'm about to choke over the fact that this boy just called what we're doing love when my home phone rings. "Hold that thought," I say as I leap up to grab it, more out of habit than necessity.

"Hello?"

"Zora?" I recognize the voice.

"Hello, Mackenzie. How are you?"

"I'm okay."

"You sound sad. What's wrong?"

She tells me about her aunt, and her mother, and the whole breakup with Dino and how she's going to miss the pageant for a job interview.

"Wow, sounds like you've got a hell of a lot on your plate right now," I say.

"I'm sorry. I didn't call to weigh you down with all my stuff," she says. "I totally didn't mean to do that."

"Don't worry about it."

"I was actually calling for your advice on what you think I should wear to the job interview – you know, with the newspaper."

"Right, right." I think about her options. "You don't want to look corporate. I've never met a photojournalist who looks corporate. And you don't want to look too young and silly, either. You want to look like a serious photographer without looking like you take yourself too seriously."

"If you don't want to help me with this I can totally figure it out myself," she says. "I shouldn't have bothered you."

"Stop that, Mackenzie. Right now. Quit apologizing for yourself."

She gasps.

"What?" I ask.

"That's so weird."

"What is?"

"That's exactly what my aunt always says."

"Rosie?"

"Yes."

"Then you should take her advice. Here's my suggestion. You wear dark slacks, like something from Ann Taylor, only from the more casual side, definitely not a suit pant."

"Okay."

"Even a trouser jean would work, if it's dark enough."

"Okay."

"Get some nice shoes, but make sure they're flat and comfortable."

"Really?"

"I saw a documentary on journalism once and the part that I've always remembered talked about how journalists have to be ready to run. I think it was Helen Thomas or someone like that, talking about how they tell the real reporters from the fancy ones, especially with women. Real reporters wear comfortable shoes because they know that when news breaks they're going to probably have to run and climb over things."

"Comfortable...flats..."

I think she's writing this shit down. I smile.

"But not ugly. Marc Jacobs usually has some great flats. That might be too showy, though. Maybe more like Tod's. They've got classic-looking flats with just a little bit of an edge. That's what I think you want."

"A...bit of...an...edge."

"Like a splash of color. Something comfortable and practical, but edgy."

"Splash of color. Practical. Edgy."

"To show that you've got an eye for design but that you also understand the requirements of the job."

"Okay."

"And for a top, I think you should do something kind of tailored but not too showy. Like a nice classic button-down shirt in a great color, over a silk T-shirt. Maybe a practical necklace of some kind. I'm thinking a Robert Graham shirt, maybe stripes, and a nice little matching sweater, but not too preppy or precious. You don't want to look too sweet to do damage. You know what I mean?"

I sigh.   "I think so."

"You're already pretty and petite. You don't want to give them more reason to think you might not be strong enough to do the job. So forget the stripes. Go for bold solids, dark colors. You're so damn feminine, come to think of it, you might even want to think you're kind of dressing in drag."

"Like masculine."

"Kind of. But without being dowdy."

"Okay."

"You know what I mean?" I ask.

"I do. I have it. I know what to wear now. You really saved me."

"Yeah? What were you thinking of wearing before?"

"A pink suit."

"Ha-ha!"

"I was serious."

"Oh, lord. Don't lose my number, MacKenzie. You need me."

"I know it."

There's a pause in the conversation and it seems like neither of us can think of the right thing to say.

Finally, I speak. "I want to thank you, Mackenzie."

"For what?"

"You probably don't realize this, but you've helped me a lot, too."

"How?"

Yardbird walks into the kitchen wearing nothing but his boxers, and looking mighty fine in them at that.

"I can't talk about it right now," I say, thinking this little girl actually helped me realize that I made a huge mistake when I was young and in love, and I've been paying for it ever since, but she also made me realize it was okay to take a chance now and then, to try something new, to move past other people's expectations of you. To be unafraid to do what you want even if it doesn't seem like anyone will think it's wise.

"Am I catching you at a bad time?" she asks as Yardbird slips his hands around my waist from behind, and kisses my left shoulder.

"No," I say, leaning into his body. "You're actually catching me at the best time I can remember in a while. But I can't talk right now. I'll call you later."

I hang up the phone and turn to face Yardbird. We kiss. I think about asking him about that love word he used back in the bedroom a little while ago, but the moment is gone. I choose instead to just exist in this man's embrace, feeling the truth of what he said without having to speak it yet myself.

Mackenzie

I've never been this nervous. Even in front of a packed stadium. Even on a pageant stage during the swimsuit competition. I stand alone in the elevator, heading up to the photo editor's floor, and look at my reflection in the metal of the door.

I've got on funky black flats, black casual cotton slacks, a pale green button-down shirt over a silk T-shirt in the same shade, and a small, simple silver chain necklace and small matching hoop earrings. I've got my hair twisted into a neat knot at the base of my neck, and a plain black Coach briefcase – my one splurge item – hangs off my shoulder.

The elevator stops, dings, and the doors slide open. Waiting for me is a woman who looks younger than I expected, with mocha skin and loose, long curls. She wears an outfit very similar to the one I wear, and I realize Zora was right about the wardrobe advice. The woman smiles to see me and steps forward. "Mackenzie?" she asks. I nod and she extends her hand to me. "Hi, welcome. I'm Natalie Cooper."

"Nice to meet you, Natalie."

She smiles and says, "Please, follow me."

Natalie leads me down the hall, past dozens of desks in a large, open area – the newsroom. A lot of people have phones to their ears, busy at work, typing. A few people run here and there, talking animatedly with one another. So much excitement!

"This is one of our newsrooms," says Natalie. "Photo is just down the way over here. May I get you something to drink? Water? Coffee?"

"No, thank you."

I follow her and feel completely and totally like a fraud. I don't know why I'm here. It's weird. But I remind myself that I'm doing this for Rosie. Unsurprisingly, my mother did not even speak to me today, pouting over the missed opportunity of the beauty pageant. My father wished me luck, though, and the tension between the two of them was obvious.

"Here we are," says Natalie. She stands in the doorway to a small, cozy office and motions me in. I enter and take the seat across from the desk. Framed photos occupy nearly every inch of wall space, many with signatures on them. I don't know what to do with my hands. I consciously rest them on the arms of the chair and try to seem relaxed. Natalie sits at the desk, puts on a pair of trendy-looking eyeglasses, and looks at my resume on her desk. Rosie seems to have done a very professional job on it.

"So," says Natalie as she looks up, removes the reading glasses and smiles at me, "You're a professional cheerleader?" She seems like this is hard for her to believe, like she thinks it's some kind of joke.

"For three years now."

"Tell me. What do the women on the team think of your work?"

"You mean the cheerleader series?"

She nods.

"They've never seen it. I'd have to be crazy to let them see it."

"Surely they see you taking photos?"

"I tell them it's for scrap-booking."

Natalie narrows her eyes at me as if she thinks I'm sneaky and smart. "I see. And what do you think they'd think if we wanted to run the series in the paper?"

"You mean the Chronicle?"

Natalie laughs at me. "I don't work for any other newspaper."

"I don't think that would be a good idea."

She seems surprised. "Why not?"

"I'd lose my job."

"The cheering job?"

"Yeah."

"What if you got another job?"

"I have another job, teaching dance at Mariposa High School."

Natalie gives a perfunctory look at the resume, then looks up at me. "I mean, what if I offered you a job here, Mackenzie? Would you be willing to let us run the cheerleader series?"

I gasp without meaning to. "A job?"

"I can only offer you the summer internship officially at this point," she says apologetically. "And I'm absolutely ready to do that. You're by far the best candidate we have. We've talked to quite a few people, but yours is the work that stays with me. But I want you to understand one of our staff members is leaving after that for two years, and we'd be looking for a replacement for that time period."

"I see."

"And if you did as good a job over the course of the internship as you've done in the sample photos you've sent in, I'd have to say you'd have a pretty good shot of staying on with us. At least for those two years. And who knows what might happen after that."

"I see."

"Newspapers are like professional sports."

"God, I hope not," I joke.

Natalie smiles. "What I mean is, players come, players go. We're always trading our players to other papers. There's a lot of movement in this business."

"Right."

"Anyway, we'd like to run this series soon. We could do it this weekend. If you let us, of course. We'd pay you freelance for it. Oh, by the way, did you remember to bring any other work with you?" she asks. "I'm dying to see what else you can do with that eye of yours."

"Yes, right here."

I take the series of shots I've done of Mariposa High School, and slide it across the desk to her. "This is something I'm pretty passionate about," I say. "The state of the schools in the East End."

She opens to the first page. It's a photo of a young man trying to read Chaucer in a trash-strewn courtyard while a couple of other students light up a marijuana cigarette nearby. He wears a tie and glasses, and seems terribly out of place among the gang-bangers who tease him in the background.

"I call that one 'The Man of Law,'" I say.

Natalie's eyes flash with excitement. "Isn't that the name of a Chaucer story?"

"Yes."

"Very clever! I love it. You hardly ever see these kinds of kids, you know," she seems awkward for a moment. "Mexican kids – no offense – portrayed like this."

"They're not all Mexican," I say. "Some of them are from Central America, too. And most were born here. So they're Americans, not Mexicans."

"Really?" She seems genuinely surprised by this. She flips through the whole book, nodding at just about every shot. She looks up when she finishes it. "What was the point of the series?" she asks. "I mean, if someone asked you, how would you explain it to someone?"

"To show the Herculean efforts it takes for these children to be normal students in abnormal circumstances."

"Excellent," she says, nodding in agreement. "I love it." She glances at a few of the photos again. "I assume this the school where you teach?"

I nod.

"How would you feel about us running this series, too, maybe in the Sunday magazine, as a photo essay with first-person text by you."

"I guess I'm just setting myself up to lose all my jobs," I say, jokingly. Natalie doesn't laugh.

"Sometimes you have to lose something to realize you were actually meant to have something else."

For some reason I think of Rosie, and try to stop my eyes from filling with tears. The sense of Rosie's presence in the room is almost overwhelming. I'm doing this because she asked me to, I remind myself. Even if it means losing the jobs I've got. I try to think of someone to take my place teaching the Mariposa girls dance team. There are a couple of girls on the Ranchers team who come to mind. I'll have to find a way to ask them without getting them in trouble for the crime of speaking to a photographer who had the audacity to show them as human beings rather than as perfect little Barbie dolls.

"So you'd be okay with us running both of these series?"

I shake myself out of my spooked sense, and nod. "Yes, of course, but do you really think they're good?"

Natalie looks at me as if I've asked an absurd question. "You don't see it?"

"I don't know. I never really thought something that was fun and easy could qualify as work. And I don't exactly come from a family that thinks taking pictures is the kind of thing you do for work."

I hope she's not offended by what I've said.

Natalie looks at me for a long time, and says, "All that means is that you're a born photographer, Mackenzie. I'd like you to start next week if you're ready."

"So soon?"

"Our normal internship cycle doesn't start for another month, but we've got a little extra money in the budget, and we've got a team heading to Haiti to cover some reconstruction issues there. I'd love to get you in on that if you're willing."

"Haiti?"

"I'm excited to see what you'd do there."

"Okay."

"I call it baptism by fire."

"Okay," I say.

Natalie leans back in her chair. "Well," she says, looking pleased with herself. "Now that we've got that out of the way, tell me a little more about yourself."

I take a deep breath and try to stop my heart from making so much noise. "I guess I'm just your normal Texan girl," I begin. "It's just that I like to take pictures."

After the interview I drive straight to the hospital to share the good news with Rosie. I practically skip down the hall toward her room. I round the corner with a huge grin on my face, more excited to tell her she was right all along than I've ever been to tell my own mother I won a pageant or made a cheer squad.

"You'll never guess what happened today," I call as I waltz into the room. But Rosie's not there. No one is in the room. The bed sits empty, without sheets. My heart begins to bang again as I zip through the room, and out into the hall again. "Rosie?" I race down the hall toward the nurses' station. The two women there look up at me, and then at each other with sad, guilty eyes.

"Where's Rosie?" I ask.

"Who?"

"Rosalba Morales," I say. "She's my aunt. What happened to her? She was in that room right there, and now she's gone."

The nurses look at each other again, and the shorter, stouter one steps forward and takes my hands in hers. "I'm sorry," she says. "Your aunt passed away a little less than an hour ago."

Zora

Yardbird leaves my apartment on Sunday morning, and calls me as soon as he arrives back in Houston.

"What did you say the name of that crazy little cheerleader was again?" he asks.

"Mackenzie something-or-other, Spanish name," I say. "Why?"

Yardbird laughs out loud. "Well, I just got home and brought in my Sunday paper, and opened it up and there were all these photos of cheerleaders, a whole series of them in black and white, only they look like crazy professional athlete photos, with the blood, sweat and tears and the whole thing. They don't look like the way cheerleaders usually look in pictures."

"And? Was her picture there?"

"Her name Mackenzie de la Garza?" he asks.

"Yeah, that's it."

"She took the damn pictures," he says.

"She what?"

"It says right here, 'photos by Mackenzie de la Garza.' She wrote some text that says she recently left the team to take an internship at the Chronicle, and that these are the most candid unguarded shots ever published of professional cheerleaders."

"Do they look good?" I ask.

"They're damn good, girl."

I tell him to call me back later, and then I rush down to the corner newsstand to see if they have a copy of the Houston Chronicle.

Life is full of surprises.

Mackenzie

Justin lives in a one-bedroom loft apartment in downtown Houston. I've left my car at the hospital, in the parking lot. Justin came to see Rosie shortly after the nurses told me she had died. At first he offered to take me home, because it was obvious to everyone I was in no shape to drive. But I didn't want to go home. I didn't want to have to deal with my parents. Their house doesn't feel like home to me anymore anyway. I told Justin I just wanted to see Rosie, and it was he who suggested I come with him here to his place to calm down. "I'll make you some tea, and we'll just talk for a while," he said.

I follow him through the underground parking lot to the bank of elevators now, numb on my feet, unable to believe what's happening. Justin doesn't try to talk to me yet. He just offers a steady hand on my elbow to guide me.

The apartment is small and modern, crammed with books from the floor to the ceiling, and I'm surprised that he has a cat. Dino hated cats, and joked about how he'd like to practice hunting on the ones that wandered around his parents' neighborhood. I'd always assumed all men disliked cats.

"This is Frida," he says as the cat approaches and rubs herself across my ankles. "She's still waiting for her Diego."

269

Justin leads me to a light blue leather sofa, and settles me in. I still can't think of anything to say.

"I'll just make some tea," he says.

I check out the titles of the books in a pile on the glass coffee table. Brownsville: Stories, by Oscar Casares. Crazy Loco, by David Talbot Rice. The Jumping Tree, by Rene Saldaña Jr. I've never heard of any of these writers.

"Here you go," say Justin, setting my tea down on the coffee table next to the stack of books.

"Thank you," I manage. I don't feel like drinking anything, but take the warm cup into my hands. I feel so cold. Outside is hot and humid, of course, but Rosie's death has left me chilled to the bone. Justin picks out one of the books from the stack. The cover is red and yellow, bright, with a distinctive Mexican influence to the design, including a skull. He hands the book to me. I read the title. The Tequila Worm, by Viola Cañales.

"Rosie gave me this," he says.

"Really?"

Justin smiles sorrowfully. "She had good taste in books," he says. "It's a great book. It's for teenagers, but Rosie said she identified with the girl in it."

I hold it and try to imagine Rosie reading it.

"You can keep it," he says.

"But she gave it to you," I protest.

"I want you to have it."

I hold the book to my chest, cradle it, and begin to cry again. Justin sits next to me on the sofa and wraps his arms around me. He says nothing, just holds me and rocks gently.

"I had something to tell her," I say. "And now I can't."

"Shh," he says. "It's okay."

"It's not okay!"

"You're right, it's not okay. It's terrible. Rosie was one of the best people I've ever met."

"I wanted to tell her," I repeat.

"What did you have to tell her?"

I tell Justin about the internship, and he stops holding me. "That's fantastic news, Mackenzie!"

I cannot stop crying. "But I wanted to tell Rosie. It would have made her so happy. She would have been proud of me."

Justin shakes his head. "She was already proud of you. Don't you know that? All she could do was brag about you. If she'd had her own daughter there's no way she could have loved her more than she loved you. She was crazy about you, and she knew you'd get the job at the paper."

I nod and sniffle. He hands me a box of tissue and rubs my back gently.

"That's what she said. She never had any doubt."

"I wanted to tell her, that's all." I feel my face screw up with the tears.

"Knowing Rosie, she's listening in on us right now," says Justin. "Tell her now."

And so I do.

Zora

I walk into the lobby of my offices and greet the receptionist.

"Welcome back, Miss Jackson!" she cries with entirely too much enthusiasm. "You look well-rested."

"I am. Is Tara in yet?"

"Yes, ma'am. She's been here for about an hour."

"Thank you."

I walk with purpose down the hallway toward my corner office, waving and greeting those who must be waved to and greeted.

At the end of the hall, Tara sits at her desk in the waiting area outside of my office, puzzling over something written on a notebook. She looks up as I approach.

"Miss Jackson! Welcome back. How was Houston?"

"Wonderful," I say. Normally, I would simply take messages from Tara, bark some orders at her, and close myself up in my office. But today I want to live in the moment and really look at her, at the surroundings. I notice she has a picture in a frame on the desk. I know for a fact I would never have noticed something like that before. "Who's the baby?"

Tara seems startled by the question. She looks at me in momentary confusion, then lifts the frame in her hand, running a finger tenderly over the smiling baby's face.

"Megan. My Goddaughter," she tells me.

"I didn't know you had a Goddaughter!"

"Yeah, well I guess we never talked about it. She's my third godchild, actually." Tara produces a photo file from her purse and I stop myself from finding this annoying, as I might have not too long ago. Yardbird thinks every connection we make with every person in our lives can be meaningful and useful to us on a spiritual level, and he has asked me to try slowing down and seeing what I might learn by listening more and writing fewer lists. "This is Casandra, she's five, and that's Jessie, he's two."

"They're adorable," I say, and I mean it. Normally I would not have been able to stop worrying about the next deal or phone call enough to focus on the details of the children in the photographs. I would have gone through the motions and hurried away, annoyed that someone had taken up so much of my time with something I would have thought was trivial. Not today. Today I try to imagine, really imagine, what it feels like to be the godmother to these children. One thing MacKenzie taught me is it's a mistake to assume anyone's trivial.

"Thanks," says Tara, smiling in a way I don't think I've ever seen her smile before. "Their mom is one of my best friends from childhood. Tanya. She's got an amazing husband and they're so happy. The new baby looks just like her."

"Three babies under five," I say, impressed. "I can't imagine how she does it. It's a lot of work just having one."

Tara looks at me in what almost seems like deep thought. "You look different," she comments.

"You think?"

"Yeah, there's something about you." She pauses, thinking. "I hope you don't take this the wrong way, Miss Jackson, but you look happy."

I'm shocked by the directness of what she says. I fight the old Zora's urge to tell her to mind her own business and keep her judgments to herself. I try to understand the real point of what this woman and human being is saying to me. "You know what? I am happy, Tara."

"Things are good?"

"Things are very good," I tell her.

Tara hands me a thick stack of pink phone message slips. "I'm glad. You've got a lot of catching up to do around here. Let me know what you need me to do."

I thank her, and take the stack of messages into my office. I close the door, sit at my desk, and spread them out. I turn on my computer, and check my email inboxes. Hundreds of messages await my attention. I don't open them just yet. Instead, I log in to my stock account, and check my portfolio. Looking good. I take out a pen and a calculator and start to do the math. I've got enough invested that I could actually live off the interest alone, if I was frugal, for the rest of my life. Yardbird was right. I'm running to catch up to a finish line that I already passed. I just don't know how to stop. His theory is that I can't stop until I remember what it was that set me running in the first place. The answer to that is easy. Poverty, and the love of Ivan Barbosa. I wanted to escape the constant needs of my childhood, and then I wanted to be good enough, successful enough, that Ivan might want to change, that he might find me incredibly powerful and irresistible. It hits me all at once, the fact that I don't need to move this fast if I don't want to. I can slow down. Ivan will never love me properly, not because I'm unlovable but because he doesn't have the emotional tools to know what proper love looks like. And I'm not poor anymore. If unless I really screw things up somehow, I will never be poor again.

"So why the hell am I still running?" I ask myself.

I lean back in my chair, and begin to plan. I take out a pad of paper and use the pen to start a list. I know, it's a list. Yardbird wouldn't be happy about that – unless he knew what the list said. Across the top, I write: Work I can delegate to others for a while. When I finish that list, I start another one: Places I'd like to see before I die. I have traveled a lot in my job, but I've rarely traveled for the sake of seeing a place. It's always just been dropping in, doing business, flying out. I start with Hawaii. I know, it's predictable. But aside from work, I've never really visited the place, and I've always wanted to.

I call Tara on the phone, and tell her I'd like to set up a staff meeting as soon as possible to discuss some important changes in the company. I don't tell her that the changes will mean scaling back my workday, giving my partners more responsibilities, and letting go of the need to control everything to the point that I feel out of control.

When we hang up, I return to the notepad for one last list: People I'd like to see the world with. There are only two names that come to mind. Lissette, and Yardbird.

Mackenzie

I sit with my mother, father, grandparents and other assorted relatives in Rosie's lawyer's office, listening as the details of her will are read out loud. Rosie only had a few things of any real value, and it seems she has left most of them to me, with instructions for me to move out of my parents' house and "get a life of your own already." My parents do not seem amused. My mother continues to cry or seethe at the sight of me, and she has broken her silent treatment only once, to tell me that a "cow" has won the Miss Houston pageant and that if I'd had any sense I would have entered it and been on my way to the Miss Texas contest already.

I leave the lawyer's office with the keys to Rosie's store and home, now my store and home. What am I going to do with a store? I drive to Magnolia Park, to the store, and open the door. Justin is here, working. He's been working full-time ever since Rosie died, out of respect for her. The familiar jangle of the bell on the door handle strikes me as the saddest sound I've ever heard. Everything is the same as always, with only one thing missing. Rosie.

I find Justin at the deli counter in the rear of the store, slicing ham the way Rosie used to. He washes his hands, comes out from behind the counter, and hugs me. I tell him about the meeting at the lawyer's office, and let him know I'm his boss now.

"Uh oh," he says.

"I don't know how to run a store," I tell him. "I don't know why she left it to me."

"What are you going to do?" he asks.

"I leave for Haiti this week. And the paper is planning to run the series on the high school in a few weeks, so I'm going to lose that job for good."

"How do you feel about all that?"

"I know it's something I have to do, but I totally don't want to give up on those kids." I feel myself starting to cry again. This happens a lot.

Justin claps his hands together. "Hey!" he says. "What if you turned this place and Rosie's house into a dance and gymnastics center for neighborhood kids?"

I think about the idea. Look around the store trying to imagine it different. "It's not big enough."

"It doesn't have to be huge. You could have it be like a place where girls can come after school to dance. Forget the gymnastics part. Dance and cheer center."

It's a good idea. "What about your job?" I ask him.

"Please," he says with a dismissive wave of his hand. "I've got some applications out to newspapers myself. You don't think you're the only journalist in the room, do you?"

"Even the Chronicle?" I ask.

"As a matter of fact, I have an interview this week."

"No way!"

"Yes way. For an arts writer internship. Isn't that crazy?"

"I didn't know you applied!"

He bucks his head. "Ah, but neither did I. Your aunt was quite the agent."

The word makes me think of Zora Jackson, and I realize how much these two women had in common. I wish they'd had a chance to meet one another.

"Oh, my gosh," I say.

"Do you realize she'd been doing things like that for kids in this neighborhood for years?" he says.

"What do you mean?"

"Well, since she's been gone I've been here every day, all day, and you wouldn't believe the stories I've heard from people in the neighborhood. Rosie has been helping kids apply for college, she's been finding ways to get them job interviews. She ran this store, sure, but I think that was only half of what she really did around here. She was like a counselor to people. She even had this one family that she would talk to every week about their problems, like a therapist."

"Are you serious? She never told me that."

"There was a lot she never told people."

I think about the cancer. "Yeah," I say.

"So what do you think about turning this into a dance studio? That way you could coach all kinds of girls, from all different schools. You wouldn't be limited. We could call it Rosie's Place."

"We could?"

"I mean you. You could."

I smile at him. "We could offer more than dance classes," I say. "We could teach photography and writing, too."

Justin smiles. "We?"

"If you want."

"I think that would be good," he says.

"But I can't even start to think about this until I get back from Haiti."

"How long will you be there?"

"About a week they told me."

"So I'll run the store for a week, then you'll get back and we'll go on another one of our non-dates where we end up kissing or something, and we'll talk about finding people who know what the hell they're doing to help us get Rosie's Place going."

"I think I'd like that," I say. To myself I add, as long as it doesn't get too serious too fast. I am enjoying my freedom, and I don't think I want anyone to ruin that, not even Justin.

***

Days later, dad drives me to the airport. My mom still isn't speaking to me.

"How you feeling?" he asks.

"Nervous. Good."

"You'll be fine," he says.

We don't really speak again until we get to the airport, park, and dad helps me pull my suitcase to the terminal. I don't really need his help, but I don't have the heart to say no, either. He seems awkward, like he wants to say something.

"You okay?" I ask him.

Dad looks me in the eye and clears his throat. "I just want to say I'm sorry," he says.

"For what?"

"For never noticing."

"Never noticing what, dad?"

"How much you were like me."

"I am?"

Dad looks like he wants to cry. "I've been so busy with being the breadwinner that I just sort of left your raising to your mother."

"What are you talking about?"

"You're a smart woman, Mackenzie."

"Thanks, dad."

"Smarter than I think I realized."

"That's not true. Don't say that."

"That's why I'm sorry. I shouldn't have let her live through you like I did. It wasn't fair."

I look at his surgeons hands, and they're trembling. "Dad, stop it. It's okay. I'm fine."

"When I saw your photos in the newspaper I realized that there was this woman in there that I didn't even know, Mackenzie." He looks like he wants to cry.

"It's okay, dad. You've been busy."

"No, it's not okay. There was this woman I didn't even know, and she was someone I would have liked to have known sooner."

I feel my eyes flood with tears. "You mean that, dad?"

He hugs me. "Of course I do, Mackenzie. Please forgive me."

"Nothing to forgive," I say.

"You better go," he tells me, stepping back, composing himself.

"Okay, dad. Take good care of mom, okay? Tell her I love her."

He nods solemnly, and forces a bittersweet smile. "We're proud of you," he says in a way that makes me think he's going to work on getting mom to come around.

As I turn away and walk toward the security checkpoint, I feel like I'm growing taller. I don't turn back to see my father because even though the weight of his words has floored me, I don't want them to hold me down.

I am tired of people not seeing me. I am tired of everyone being surprised that I've got a soul.

I get to the gate, and stand in line to board the plane to Port au Prince. I take the window seat, and watch as the ground rolls beneath us, faster and faster, until we are up in the air, rising.

"Goodbye, Houston," I whisper. I look out at the clouds, and smile. "Hello, world."

Made in the USA
Lexington, KY
27 February 2014